"I didn't recognize you with your clothes on."

Silke gave an involuntary gasp at the outrageousness of the remark, knowing, by the speculative smiles being exchanged by two female shoppers a short distance away, that the clear timbre of Lyon's voice had reached them, at least.

"Height doesn't seem to matter when you're lying horizontal, does it?" She smiled up at him sweetly, challenge in her eyes now.

The two women moved a little closer, seemingly enthralled by the conversation.

"Not in the least." Lyon spoke loudly enough for the two women to hear again. "Shall we arrange a time for us to lie horizontal together again?"

CAROLE MORTIMER is the youngest of three children and grew up in a small English village with her parents and two brothers. She still loves nothing more than going "home" to visit her family. She herself now has three very active sons, four cats and a dog, which doesn't leave her a lot of time for hobbies! She has written over eighty romances.

Books by Carole Mortimer

HARLEQUIN PRESENTS
1657—GRACIOUS LADY
1671—RETURN ENGAGEMENT
1703—HUNTER'S MOON

Don't miss any of our special offers. Write to us at the following address for information on our newest releases.

Harlequin Reader Service
U.S.: 3010 Walden Ave., P.O. Box 1325, Buffalo, NY 14269
Canadian: P.O. Box 609, Fort Erie, Ont. L2A 5X3

CAROLE MORTIMER

War of Love

Harlequin Books

TORONTO • NEW YORK • LONDON
AMSTERDAM • PARIS • SYDNEY • HAMBURG
STOCKHOLM • ATHENS • TOKYO • MILAN
MADRID • WARSAW • BUDAPEST • AUCKLAND

ISBN 0-373-11727-2

WAR OF LOVE

Copyright © 1995 by Carole Mortimer.

First North American Publication 1995.

This edition published by arrangement with Harlequin Enterprises B.V.

® and TM are trademarks of the publisher. Trademarks indicated with
® are registered in the United States Patent and Trademark Office, the
Canadian Trade Marks Office and in other countries.

Printed in U.S.A.

CHAPTER ONE

IF ONE more opportunistic male used the excuse of patting the fluffy white tail on her bottom as a means of touching her, Silke knew she was going to scream!

The adolescent schoolboys had been bad enough, a small group of them taking much delight in tormenting her as they wandered around the store as a way of filling in time during their school holidays; Silke was positive that none of them could actually afford to buy anything in the prestigious store Buchanan's, and she had seen the store detective, under the guise of a customer, eyeing them cautiously too. Although he hadn't made any move to stop them when they had taunted Silke!

Just as he hadn't blown his cover when an old man had approached her a few minutes ago. Perhaps he had considered that Silke, after dealing with the schoolboys herself, was more than capable of dealing with him too. And she certainly had. She didn't care that the elderly man had twinkling grey eyes and a friendly smile; the way he had patted her bottom had been altogether too friendly, and had earned him a verbal rebuke of the most cutting kind!

Of course, she knew the way she was dressed was sure to provoke attention, had expected a few ribald jokes, but the familiarity was something else entirely. God, no wonder Nadine had decided she had something more important to do today; she had probably known exactly what this job was going to be like!

As it was, Silke intended having a word with her mother about the sort of——

'What the hell do you think you're doing?'

Silke spun round at the sound of that harshly accusing male voice—as quickly as she could in these stupid high-heeled shoes that went with the rest of this ridiculous costume. Whoever had chosen this bunny outfit had obviously opted for the overtly sexual rather than the cuddly, fluffy kind, and Silke was feeling very conspicuous with her long legs encased in silky black tights, and wearing a brief black bathing costume whose only similarity to a rabbit was the fluffy white pom-pom on her bottom. At least the fluffy white head with its long ears and face-mask had the advantage of covering up all of her hair and most of her face; she would hate anyone actually to recognise her wearing this costume!

And as she turned to face the owner of that grating voice she was glad of at least that amount of anonymity—because the thunderous-looking man who owned that more than cutting voice was looking—glaring!—straight at her! And, as far as she was aware, she had never seen him before. She would have remembered someone like him; he wasn't a man anyone was likely to forget in a hurry. Or slowly, either, for that matter...

He was taller than average, well over six feet, Silke would guess judging from the way he towered over her, his black hair styled severely short, thick black brows over the coldest grey eyes Silke had ever seen, and the handsomeness of the rest of his face—a long, straight nose and sculpted lips over a squarely aggressive jaw—was marred by the fierce anger of his expression. And it was directed straight at her!

Nevertheless, Silke found herself glancing over her shoulder to see if she could be mistaken in thinking she was the object of his anger, instantly knowing that she wasn't; for the moment there was a lull in the amount of people entering this section of this prestigious department store—and she was the only person in sight!

But, before she could reluctantly turn back to face the irate man, she felt the top of one of her arms clasped in a tight grip, the tray she held unbalancing precariously. 'Careful, I'm——'

'Move!' that harshly irritated voice said economically, and Silke almost fell over in those ridiculously high heels as she was dragged across the department store in the direction of the lift, in full view of everyone.

Which was remarkable in itself; none of the people shopping, or indeed the staff, seemed to be taking the slightest bit of notice of the woman in the bunny costume being physically manhandled in front of their eyes by a fiercely angry man—in fact, on closer inspection, the staff seemed to be looking the other way! Of course, they were a superior lot, Silke had quickly discovered, looking down at the interloper in their midst dressed in the revealing bunny costume. But, even so, she would have thought at least one of them might have shown a little concern for her being abducted by a complete stranger in front of them!

'Inside,' the man at Silke's side ordered grimly when she looked around desperately as the lift doors opened silently in front of them. Not that the instruction was really necessary; with that vice-like grip on her arm there wasn't much chance of her going anywhere but where this man decided that she should!

Unless she decided to scream. Her mother had assured her that she had a singing voice that would stop traffic in its tracks, so a scream should surely achieve a similar effect. Not that she had ever put the singing to the test before either, but——

'The top, Charlie,' the man at her side tersely instructed the lift attendant.

That stopped Silke in her tracks. The top floor...? That was where all the executive offices of this store were housed, where all the executives of the exclusive Buchanan stores had their offices...

Silke slowly turned to look at the man who stood so rigidly disapproving at her side, the scream in her throat dying to a strangled whimper. What could she have done wrong during her brief time on duty to have aroused the attention of one of the higher echelons of Buchanan's? She didn't think she had done——

Oh, God—the elderly man, the one she had given a verbal dressing-down a short time ago—he couldn't have complained about her behaviour, could he? His eyes had twinkled admiringly even after her verbal rebuke, but that didn't mean he hadn't thought better of the whole thing and complained to the management. Considering his behaviour, she should have been the one complaining! But that probably wasn't the way the management of Buchanan's would see it; they claimed that their staff were always polite and helpful; that, above all, 'the customer was always right'. In this case it probably wouldn't help for her to point out that she wasn't strictly one of their employees. In fact, in some ways, it was worse that she wasn't; her mother had been thrilled to get the call from Buchanan's personnel department, and would be mortified if Silke had blotted her agency's copy-book during their first job for them!

Silke looked up at the man she now knew to be one of Buchanan's executives with beseeching green eyes. 'If this has something to do with that elderly man earlier——'

'Thanks, Charlie.' As the lift doors opened he once again spoke to the lift attendant—once again ig-noring Silke, except to pull her out of the lift this time, glancing down fiercely at her feet as she stumbled yet again in the high-heeled shoes. 'If you can't walk in the damned things, then for God's sake take them off!' he barked disgustedly.

Deep colour heated her cheeks, her mouth opening with a sharp rejoinder for his arrogance—until she realised the lift doors were still open, and 'Charlie' was watching them with avid interest. And Silke wasn't about to provide any more of a floor show for him or anyone else, so she reached down with as much dignity as she could muster, to remove the of-fending—painful!—shoes.

The relief she felt at their removal was quickly for-gotten as the man at her side gave a contemptuous snort. 'Good God, girl, just how tall are you?'

Except that he was obviously an executive of the Buchanan group of world-exclusive stores, Silke still didn't know who this man was, but even the little she did know about him didn't give him the right to be personally offensive about her lack of height. She knew she was short—it had been the bane of her youth to realise she had stopped growing at only five feet tall—and she had told her mother she was going to look ridiculous dressed up as a bunny girl; most of the ones she had seen or read about were about six feet tall! But her mother had insisted that her lack of height would just give her a cute and cuddly look. If this man's reaction was anything to go by, it was the last thing she looked; he couldn't have been this offensive to someone who looked 'cute and cuddly'!

Silke stuck her chin out defensively, instantly realising how futile the action was; this man couldn't even see her chin behind the stupid rabbit mask, let alone that she was outraged.

'Tall enough!' she snapped, at once impatient with the stupidity of her words as much as with the ridiculous costume she was wearing. Tall enough for what? she thought self-disgustedly.

The man she had addressed the remark to obviously thought her retort was ridiculous too as he looked scornfully down his haughty nose at her!

Anything else she might have added in her defence was forgotten as she realised they were standing outside the personnel manager's office. She had been sent up to Doug Moore's office this morning when she had reported for work, and despite this arrogant man's familiarity as he marched straight past the secretary in the outer office without so much as the politeness of acknowledging her existence, and into the personnel manager's office itself, Silke knew that this man certainly wasn't Doug Moore. Doug was a tall slender man, with slightly over-long blond hair, and a manner that was more than a little flirtatious.

A man Silke had known without a doubt she could deal with. Which was more than could be said for this other man! Although that wasn't to say she wasn't going to try...

But at the moment he was far from impressed by the fact that Doug Moore wasn't in his office, turning abruptly on his well-shod heel to go back into the outer office, Silke still firmly clasped at his side, to speak to the now open-mouthed secretary.

'Find Doug and send him to my office,' he barked without preamble, not even pausing on his way out of the room to see if the poor woman had acknowledged his instruction.

And no wonder; it had been in the form of a royal command, Silke thought disgustedly, not in the least surprised, when she chanced to glance back, to see that the secretary had already picked up the telephone, obviously calling round in search of her boss. As ordered.

Really, this man, whoever he was, thought he was a one-man army, his orders to be obeyed without question. And, quite frankly, Silke had had enough.

'Look, I don't know who you are,' she told him exasperatedly, attempting to pull out of his grasp, failing miserably, only succeeding in bruising her arm even further as his fingers merely tightened their vice-like grip. She was still being pulled unceremoniously down the luxuriously carpeted hallway towards what she supposed was this man's own office. She took a deep, controlling breath, determined not to appear to be intimidated by this man. Even if she was! 'But——'

'No, you don't, do you?' the man bit out grimly, grey eyes narrowed ominously. 'But I know who you are. Or at least what you're supposed to be.' He sounded angry again now. 'You fall far short of requirements!'

She had told her mother herself that she was far too short and slight to be a bunny girl, but there was no need for this man to be continually insulting about her lack of assets!

'Now look,' she spluttered again, intending to tell him exactly what she thought of his opinion. And what he could do with it!

'I have.' As if to prove his point, he gave another disparaging glance down the slender length of her body in the revealing outfit. 'And so has every customer who entered the store this morning! Are you Doug's latest girlfriend, is that it?' he scorned, sculptured mouth twisted derisively. 'It's difficult to tell what you look like under that ridiculous rabbit head, but I suppose you could be pretty. And I know Doug's tastes run to the youthfully nubile, so I suppose it's possible that could be the explanation. It isn't an acceptable one. To me,' he added harshly. 'But it's the only one I can think of for the moment.'

Silke was once again rendered speechless; the arrogance of the man! 'Could be pretty'! 'Youthfully nubile'! The chauvinistic—— And then she remembered what she was—or rather, wasn't!—wearing, and knew there was really no defence she could offer to this man's scorn when she gave every appearance of being a half-dressed bunny girl!

She barely had time to register the comfort of the next outer office he dragged her through, without stopping, before entering the even plusher office beyond—obviously his own—before she spotted the elderly man of earlier sitting in one of the leather armchairs that faced the imposing desk, the hazy smoke from the cigar he was puffing on with enjoyment filling the room. Silke's nose—behind the rabbit mask—wrinkled with distaste at the foul-smelling weed.

But at least she had her explanation now; this old man had complained about her verbal rebuke earlier. She couldn't help wondering what explanation he had given for having earned such a rebuke; she doubted he had told the other man of the way he had touched her bottom with such familiarity.

'I took the liberty of helping myself to one of your cigars—oh, I say, Lyon.' The older man's eyes widened with enjoyment as he spotted Silke at Lyon's side—what a name! And yet somehow it fitted the man's fierceness exactly. 'I know I said she was an appealing little thing, plenty of fire, but you didn't have to bring her up here to meet——'

'Shut up, Uncle Henry,' the man who still held Silke rasped wearily. 'Sit,' he instructed her curtly, nodding in the direction of the second chair that faced the opulence of the brown leather-topped mahogany desk, around which he now moved to sit in yet another leather chair, a swivel one this time, leaning forward once he had done so, resting his arms on the leather top, his narrowed, steely gaze fixed on her steadily.

Uncle Henry! So she had made the mistake of actually snapping indignantly at this man's uncle. That explained a lot. Perhaps she should have realised before now that the two of them were related; they both had those unusual grey eyes, and they were both arrogant enough in their own way! 'Uncle Henry' had touched her earlier as if he had a perfect right to do so, and his nephew had dragged her up here without explanation just as if he had as much right. God, what a family!

'No need to take that tone with me, Lyon,' Uncle Henry told him without rancour. 'I've told you before, it has little effect when I've looked after you since you were a baby; bounced you on my knee, held you when you cried, wiped your nose for you, changed your——'

'That last claim is definitely a figment of your imagination, Uncle Henry,' the younger man cut in harshly. 'You employed a nanny for that particular task. In fact——' his mouth twisted scornfully—did it ever do anything else? Silke wondered, looking at him '—I don't remember too much of the "knee-bouncing" either; you were always too busy following your own interests!'

His uncle looked unconcerned. 'Businesses don't run themselves.' He shrugged.

'I wasn't referring to those sorts of interests,' Lyon told him drily.

The older man grinned, grey eyes—eyes the same colour as his nephew's, but oh, so different in expression!—twinkling merrily. 'So many beautiful women in the world, and so few years to enjoy them! You should try it some time, Lyon; it might make all the difference——'

'That's enough, Henry!' the younger man snapped tautly, eyes glacial now as he turned his attention back to Silke.

Which she instantly wished he hadn't. She had been finding the two men's confrontation enlightening to say the least, but it certainly hadn't improved Lyon's temper—and it was now directed back at her!

Well, if he had brought her up here, as she suspected he had, to reprimand her for her behaviour towards his uncle earlier, then he could go ahead and do it—and after he had, she would tell him exactly what a dirty old man she thought his uncle to be. And from the brief conversation between the two men just now, that shouldn't come as too much of a surprise to him! In fact, attack was her best defence, and she would get in her opinion of his uncle before he could even start on her.

'I don't know what your uncle has told you happened downstairs earlier, but——'

'I thought I told you to sit,' Lyon observed softly— too softly, dangerously so—completely ignoring her words. Again.

Which Silke was becoming more than a little tired of! 'I may be wearing this ridiculous bunny outfit——' her eyes flashed deeply green behind the mask '—but underneath this I'm a person, not an animal to be ordered about!' She was breathing deeply in her agitation.

'I'm glad you agree that what you're wearing is— inappropriate,' he rasped drily, again ignoring what she had really said. 'If you would care to re-move——'

'I don't care to remove anything!' she cut in frus-tratedly. 'And if you can't control the way your uncle behaves towards women, no matter what they are wearing, then I suggest you keep him away from them. Preferably far away!' she snapped, looking from him to his mildly surprised uncle, before once again turning back to the younger man. 'The few sharp words I said to him earlier were well deserved, and I would do it again given the same circumstances.' She glared pointedly at the older man.

Lyon was now looking at his uncle too. 'Circum-stances?' he prompted softly, dark brows raised questioningly.

The older man looked a little uncomfortable now. 'Well, as I said, Lyon, she's an appealing little thing.'

He moved his hands dismissively, once again billowing smoke around the room from the half-smoked cigar he still held.

'And, being the old rogue that you are, you couldn't resist the appeal!' his nephew realised, shaking his head disgustedly. 'God, Henry, you really are——' He broke off abruptly as the intercom buzzed on his desk. 'Yes?' he rasped impatiently into the innocent machine.

'Mr Moore to see you, Mr Buchanan,' came the disembodied voice of his secretary.

Silke missed the rest of the conversation, staring at the man who sat so confidently across the desk from her, at last beginning to realise exactly why he was so confident. Mr Buchanan! This man, the man who had forcibly dragged her into the lift and up to the executive floor of the department store, was a *Buchanan*.

My God, and not just any Buchanan, from the way he had behaved towards her from the first and the deference with which the staff had treated him, but Buchanan himself, the owner of the store! Unless he was the son; she had thought the owner of the Buchanan group was someone called Charles Buchanan. Although this man's uncle had said he had effectively been Lyon Buchanan's guardian since he was a baby, so... None of this really made any difference to the fact that this man was a Buchanan. And the man she had verbally rebuked earlier was his uncle!

She didn't need any further telling to sit down; she almost fell into the waiting chair. What a mess! And her mother...! Oh, God, what her mother was going to say about this she just didn't like to think.

Silke turned dazedly as the office door opened behind them to admit Doug Moore.

'Ah, Doug, so glad you could join us at last,' he told the other man silkily now, getting slowly to his feet, instantly putting his personnel manager at a disadvantage with his superior height—if he needed any added advantage. His position as owner of the store already more than gave him that!

The younger man looked puzzled by his employer's obvious displeasure—obvious, despite the pleasantness of his tone; there was an air of menace about Lyon Buchanan that was unmistakable. 'I was down in Ladies' Fashions when I got your message——'

'A pity you didn't pay Confectionery a visit some time this morning,' Lyon Buchanan told him icily. 'Would you like to tell me what that is?'

'That' was Silke!

She had recovered enough from the shock of realising exactly who this man was to look up to see what Lyon Buchanan was talking about, only to discover he was looking directly at her. *She* was 'that'. Her shock was replaced by indignation as she realised he was once again talking about her as if she weren't a person, with feelings, but an object to be discussed. And she didn't care who he was, he still had no right——

'Good God!' Doug Moore, the man who had been perfectly charming to her earlier this morning when they met—probably because of his penchant for 'pretty, youthful nubiles'—was now looking at her with something approaching horror. 'I—my God...!' he said again, weakly this time, looking in need of a chair himself now. Except that there wasn't another one available!

'A bunny girl, Doug,' Lyon Buchanan rasped with feeling. 'You employed a damned *bunny girl* in a costume so revealing that every lecher within a hundred miles made a beeline for her.' He looked pointedly at his uncle. 'A bunny girl,' he repeated again, as if he could still hardly believe it, 'to give away our line of chocolate Easter bunnies. When it should have been a cute fluffy rabbit children would find appealing!'

At last Silke was being given an insight into exactly why she had been dragged off the shop floor and up here to the office of Lyon Buchanan himself—and it had nothing to do with what she had said to his uncle Henry! She had wondered at his puzzlement earlier concerning her accusations towards his uncle; now she knew it was because he had had no idea of the verbal encounter between his Uncle Henry and herself; the way his uncle had informed him she was dressed appeared to be the problem!

'Forgive me if I'm wrong, Doug,' Lyon Buchanan continued smoothly—his tone saying he knew damn well he wasn't the one in the wrong, that he rarely, if ever, was! 'But I thought we had agreed, during the meeting concerning this particular promotion, that we would contact an agency and take on someone who would——'

'Wear a cute, fluffy bunny costume while giving away the chocolates,' Doug Moore finished weakly, staring at Silke in the revealing costume as if he still couldn't quite believe his eyes. 'I don't understand how the mistake could have happened——'

'Oh, you admit there's been a mistake?' his employer prompted with raised brows, still supremely confident in the mistake's not being of his making.

Just as Silke was. But she wasn't sure it was completely Doug Moore's either; the instructions her mother had received had been ambiguous to say the least—a simple request for a girl in a bunny costume to promote a line at the store. And when Silke had reported to Doug Moore this morning she hadn't been in costume, had changed in the staff-room later, so neither of them had realised then that the mistake had been made. And that appeared to be what this was: a genuine mistake, brought about through lack of information on both sides.

Although from the look of increasing anger on Lyon Buchanan's face he wasn't going to be satisfied with that explanation! But it was the truth, so what more could any of them say?

'Buchanan's has a reputation to uphold,' he told his personnel manager icily. 'And I don't believe having a barely clothed bunny girl in fishnet tights parading around the store is quite the image——'

'I'm not wearing fishnet tights!' Silke cut in indignantly as she stood up; she had drawn the line at that part of the costume that had been supplied to her, preferring to wear her own sheer black tights. Not much of an improvement, she knew, when the entire length of her legs was visible, but it was better than those awful things that had arrived with the rented costume.

Lyon Buchanan looked down the long length of his autocratic nose at her. 'In that case, you have a series of holes in the tights you are wearing, which is just as bad——'

'What can you expect?' Silke demanded indignantly, her cheeks burning hotly from where she had looked down and realised he was right about the holes in her tights; there were at least half a dozen in the right leg, and another two on the left. And she hated ladders or holes in her tights, usually carried a spare pair around with her when she was out; but there was nowhere in the briefness of this costume that she could have put a spare pair of tights. 'After the way you manhandled me earlier——'

'Really, Lyon,' his uncle drawled drily, eyes twinkling merrily once again. 'It's good to realise you have more than the stuffy Buchanan blood running through your veins after all; that you found the young lady's charms equally——'

'Don't be more ridiculous than you normally are, Henry,' Lyon Buchanan cut in impatiently.

'Exactly,' Silke snapped, equally unimpressed with the idea of this man's making any overt moves where she was concerned; she thought he was the most insufferable man she had ever met! 'I realise—now—that there has been some sort of mix-up concerning the sort of bunny costume you wanted——'

'Oh, you realise it too, do you?' Lyon Buchanan turned to her harshly. 'Well, I'm—for God's sake take that ridiculous head off; I refuse to carry on a conversation with a girl wearing a bunny girl costume and a rabbit's head with buck teeth!'

He didn't have to point out how stupid the white fluffy rabbit head looked, with its long floppy ears, a nose that twitched when she talked, and the unrealistically long front teeth. He didn't have to, but it was just like this man—she had quickly come to realise!—to do so!

Her face flushed with embarrassment as much as with anger, Silke reached up to release the Velcro at the back of the mask, bending her head down to peel the fluffy mask away, shaking her hair back over her shoulders as she finally looked at the three men completely as herself, Silke Jordan, her silver-blonde hair long and straight to her shoulderblades, green eyes surrounded by thick dark lashes, her nose small and straight, her mouth full and pink, her chin pointed.

The admiration she had seen on Doug Moore's face this morning returned to his eyes, and even Lyon Buchanan was looking at her with a certain amount of male assessment now. But it was the reaction of Uncle Henry—Silke didn't know what else to call him; there certainly hadn't been any opportunity for introductions!—that took them all by surprise. He took one look at Silke—and instantly collapsed back in his chair, clutching the left side of his chest, dropping the stub of his cigar on the carpeted floor as he did so!

CHAPTER TWO

SILKE had had some reactions in the past to the way she looked, the largeness of emerald-green eyes and her full pouting mouth having caused emotions from mild interest to outright lechery, depending on the man's taste in women. But she had never before known a man collapse just at the sight of her face!

The three people in the room still standing took several seconds to realise exactly what had happened, and then—predictably—Lyon Buchanan was the first to move.

'What the hell——?' He quickly reached his uncle's side, his earlier disparagement of the older man completely belied by the concern now etched into his face, grim lines beside his nose and mouth as he moved to loosen his uncle's tie and release the top button of his shirt. 'Henry!' he prompted determinedly. 'Uncle Henry!' he urged again when he received no response, reaching for his uncle's jacket now.

'I don't think you should move him.' Silke put out the cigar before going down on her haunches beside the two men.

Grey eyes were turned on her like rapiers. 'I wasn't going to!' Lyon Buchanan rasped harshly. 'I was looking for these.' He held up a bottle of pills he had taken from the inside pocket of his uncle's jacket. 'Put one of these under your tongue, Henry,' he instructed the elderly man firmly, and his uncle roused himself enough to take the pill into his mouth, the room becoming deathly still as they waited for the pill to take effect.

Pained grey eyes finally blinked open, the older man focusing on Lyon with effort. 'I—what happened?' his uncle said groggily as he began to straighten in the chair, his recovery rapid now.

Lyon Buchanan moved back slightly, the concern that had etched his face minutes before replaced by his usual cynicism. 'One bunny girl too many, I believe,' he drawled derisively, giving Silke a scathing look, his worry about his uncle's health—and Silke wasn't sure now whether or not she had imagined it!—completely gone.

And, in fact, his uncle did look completely recovered, the colour back in his cheeks, only the merriment in his eyes slightly dulled. His expression was apologetic as he once again looked at Silke. 'Sorry about that, my dear. I—I was just—surprised, when I saw you.' He gave a rueful grimace at what he now seemed to feel was an embarrassing incident.

'You don't usually react that way to a beautiful woman,' Lyon Buchanan drawled mockingly, moving to sit back behind his imposing desk. 'Perhaps age is finally catching up with you after all!'

'Don't you believe it, boy,' his uncle rallied with some of his earlier spirit. 'And don't be too hard on this young lady either.' He turned to give Silke a conspiratorial smile. 'There has obviously been a genuine mistake made. And if I had realised my coming up here to congratulate you on finally moving out of the stuffy Buchanan mould by introducing a lovely bunny girl into the store would result in this young lady's being hauled over the coals in the way that she has been, I would have kept my mouth shut.' He reached out and clasped Silke's hand. 'I'm sorry, my dear, but I don't know your name . . . ?'

Silke ignored Lyon Buchanan's scathing snort at his uncle's familiarity in holding her hand in this way, although she was ridiculous standing here in her bunny girl costume, big holes in her tights, holding the hand of a man she had considered a lecherous old devil until a short time ago.

In fact he probably still was, she decided, removing her hand to place it behind her back together with the other one. 'Silke,' she supplied huskily. 'Silke Jordan.'

'Is that for real, or a stage name?'

Her eyes flashed as she looked across at Lyon Buchanan, her pointed chin raised defensively. 'It's for real,' she snapped, stung by his derisive tone. 'I don't have a "stage name".'

He shrugged unconcernedly. 'I thought most of the people who worked for agencies like yours were out-of-work actors or actresses?'

And it was obvious what opinion he held of people in that profession! Really, 'stuffy' didn't even begin to describe this man. He looked conservative through and through, from his short-styled hair and tailored dark suit to his plain black leather shoes. The only thing that saved him from being a complete pompous ass, in Silke's eyes, was that he was so damned good-looking—arrogantly so, of course, but even that would hold a certain attraction for some women. Not Silke; she wasn't interested in any man at the moment, and hadn't been for some time. And it was obvious that Lyon Buchanan was completely unimpressed with her too, still looking at her as if she were some sort of oddity that had wandered into his ordered—stuffy!—existence. As no doubt she was. Not that she had ever thought of herself as an oddity; but to Lyon Buchanan she probably was!

And he was right about the people who worked for her mother's agency; most of them were actors and actresses momentarily 'resting'. Nadine had managed to get an audition this morning, which was the reason she had cried off this assignment at the last minute. The very last minute, calling in at the agency on her way to the audition to tell Silke's mother she couldn't be at Buchanan's today.

And as Silke had been there talking to her mother... And as Buchanan's was an important new account... Besides, the bunny girl outfit was Silke's size! As far as her mother had been concerned, no further argument was necessary!

'Most of them are,' she confirmed Lyon Buchanan's statement distantly.

Grey eyes narrowed on her in cold assessment. 'But not you?' Lyon Buchanan finally said softly.

'No, not me,' she told him dismissively—unwilling to tell him exactly what sort of an 'out-of-work' she actually was.

Besides, she wasn't out of work, she was a self-employed jewellery designer, who just hadn't managed to sell any of her designs lately!

His mouth twisted derisively. 'You do this sort of thing because you like it?'

Her cheeks became flushed at his insulting tone. 'As your uncle has so rightly pointed out, there has been a genuine mistake concerning the sort of bunny costume you wanted.' She deliberately didn't answer his challenging remark. 'If you will give me an hour to get back to the agency, I will make sure you are supplied with the cuddly fluffy kind.' And she had no intention of being inside the costume herself; had no intention of coming anywhere near Buchanan's—or Lyon Buchanan himself!—ever again! She couldn't afford the prices in a store like this anyway, had only ever window-shopped in the past when she had come in. She could easily forgo that particular pleasure for the certainty of never having to see Lyon Buchanan again!

'I don't believe we have yet ascertained just exactly whose "genuine mistake" it was,' Lyon Buchanan said hardly, shooting his personnel manager a hard, questioning look.

'Oh, for goodness' sake, Lyon.' His uncle stood up impatiently, a short, dapper man who bore little resemblance to his nephew in build—or manner. 'That really isn't important now. Allow me to drive you wherever you need to go, my dear,' he offered Silke smoothly.

She deliberately avoided looking at Lyon Buchanan as she sensed the scorn emanating from him across the room at her. 'It's very kind of you——'

'My uncle is rarely kind—unless he has an ulterior motive,' Lyon Buchanan cut in derisively now.

'Thank you, I would appreciate that,' Silke firmly accepted the offer she had had every intention of refusing until Lyon Buchanan's scathing intervention.

Did the man never stop? Of course, he probably knew his uncle better than she did, but even so she was quite capable of deciding for herself whether or not she was prepared to accept a lift from him; she didn't need the younger man's derisive interference. The fact that she now agreed to Uncle Henry's offer of a lift—she really must find out his full name!—

didn't really matter; she could easily get out of that once they had left this office.

Lyon Buchanan was now looking at her speculatively, as if he now suspected her motives in accepting the older man's offer. He would! He was a suspicious individual. Arrogant in the extreme. But he was also the owner of Buchanan's. And when she got back to the agency she would have to explain exactly how they had upset this powerful man. Silke didn't doubt for one moment that her mother's agency would never be used again by this man. Unless...

Swallowing her pride, she turned to the owner of Buchanan's with a bright, meaningless smile. 'Someone will return from the agency this afternoon when an—appropriate costume has been acquired.' Her pride wasn't dampened enough for her not to resist reminding him of the description he had given earlier for her present costume!

But considering she had actually been hired to hand out free chocolate Easter bunnies to bright-eyed, expectant children, it was probably the only description that fitted!

God, she was going to start giggling over the ridiculousness of the situation in a minute, the humour of the whole thing finally getting to her. And Lyon Buchanan didn't look as if he would be impressed by that at all!

He was looking down at her with those cold grey eyes again now. 'I'll have your agency called and let them know my decision. When I've made one,' he added pointedly.

And for the moment she would have to be satisfied with that, his tone clearly stated. Oh, well, she had tried; she certainly wasn't going to grovel to this man—not even for the sake of her mother's agency.

'And you ought to go and see your doctor.' Lyon Buchanan was talking to his uncle now as the older man turned to leave.

Henry looked irritated by the instruction. 'Don't fuss, Lyon,' he dismissed impatiently. 'As you so rightly said, it was just a question of "one bunny girl too many"!' his humour returned, his eyes twinkling mischievously as he looked at Silke.

'Nevertheless, I intend calling Peter Carruthers and making an appointment for you,' his nephew told him determinedly.

Silke could see that Henry didn't like the younger man's arrogance one little bit—did any of them?— but he didn't attempt to argue with him any further. She couldn't help wondering if many people ever had during this man's thirty-five or thirty-six years, or if that could be the reason he seemed to be a law unto himself?

'Not you, Doug,' Lyon Buchanan rasped now as his personnel manager would have followed them from the room. 'I don't believe we have finished our conversation.'

Silke felt sorry for Doug Moore—but that didn't stop her hurrying from the room as Henry held the door open for her; she didn't want again to become the focus of Lyon Buchanan's displeasure.

Unfortunately, she wasn't quick enough!

'As for you, Miss Jordan——' his voice was raised slightly as he halted her departure '—I suggest you go and cover yourself up as soon as possible.'

Her cheeks were fiery red as, after shooting him a look of resentment from flashing green eyes, she made good her escape.

Henry was chuckling as he closed the door firmly behind them.

Silke looked at him curiously, unable to see anything remotely funny about the situation.

'No wonder there isn't a woman in Lyon's life at present,' he explained his humour as they walked towards the lift. 'I had always thought it was that he'd become so jaded because most of them were only after the Buchanan money and name. But on second thoughts I think it's because he frightens them all away!'

Silke wasn't in the least interested in Lyon Buchanan's private life—or lack of it! As far as she was concerned, she never wanted to see the man again! And yet at the same time this elderly man's description of Lyon's cynicism where women were concerned evoked a very lonely life for the younger man. Although looking at him, the stern handsomeness of his face, his lithe body beneath the tailored suit, Silke couldn't see him, jaded or not, being without some sort of female companionship in his life. And if he didn't have a woman in his life it was obviously of his own choosing, so she certainly shouldn't be feeling sorry for the man. My God, what did she have to feel sorry for Lyon Buchanan for? He was a man who had everything, looks, power, money. And if there was no woman in his life, as his uncle seemed to be claiming, then it *had* to be because he frightened them away!

'Silke is a very unusual name, my dear,' Lyon Buchanan's uncle prompted softly as they made their descent in the lift.

She shrugged dismissively. 'My mother chose it.' It wasn't something she had ever really questioned; it was just her given name.

'It's very pretty.' Henry nodded, his expression thoughtful. 'Your mother must be an unusual woman...?'

'Unusual' described her mother exactly, Silke acknowledged ruefully. She hadn't met and married Silke's father until she was twenty-seven, and before that time she seemed to have travelled the world, doing all sorts of casual jobs, having no responsibilities except to support herself. Which she seemed to have done quite capably.

Silke's father had been a rancher in Colorado, and the marriage between the two only seemed to have lasted long enough for them to have produced Silke, after which Silke's mother had gone off on her travels again, this time with Silke on her back. Silke's relationship with her father had been nil once they had left the ranch, Jack Jordan seeming to have washed his hands of both of them once the decision to go had been made.

Silke's childhood had been a succession of temporary homes and schools, until at thirteen her father had died and left her a legacy that enabled her mother to send her to boarding school. It was the first settled home Silke had ever known, and despite missing her wanderlust mother she had revelled in the stability she found there.

As her mother had revelled in her new-found freedom, travelling more than ever, always one step ahead of being tied down to any one place, or person. How long this agency would last, Silke had no idea, although she had to admit her mother seemed to find the variety of running an agency like Jordan's Miracles exciting, and its success couldn't be doubted, having gained a very creditable reputation in the year it had been open.

Silke couldn't help wondering if that would still be true after today's blunder!

'Something like that,' Silke answered the elderly man non-committally. 'Look, thank you for the offer of a lift back to the agency.' She turned to him once they were on the ground floor of the department store. 'But——'

'But you only accepted to put my nephew firmly in his place,' Henry acknowledged ruefully, eyes twinkling sympathetically for the awkward situation she had found herself in—something Lyon Buchanan didn't seem to appreciate at all! But then, why should he? As far as he was concerned, dressed as she was, she had just dragged his store down to a level he found intolerable.

A delicate blush darkened her cheeks at the elderly man's astuteness. 'I have to go and change into my own clothes before I leave, and——'

'As Lyon instructed?' Henry taunted softly.

Her chin went up defensively. 'No, not as he instructed! I have no wish to be seen out in public dressed like this either,' she added disgustedly.

Henry looked at her appreciatively. 'I think it's rather—fetching.'

She knew exactly what he thought, had been left in no doubt of that earlier. But his view of her appearance just enhanced her desire to be back in the comfort of her own clothes. 'If you'll excuse me——'

'I'm going to wait for you, Silke,' he told her firmly.

She frowned at his determined expression. 'I don't think——'

'My car will be waiting outside for you, my dear.' The laughter had gone from his eyes now as the impression of a flirtatious elderly man was erased by the intensity of his expression.

Silke looked at him frowningly. What a strange family these two men were; she couldn't work them out at all.

But she did know that both of them were too fond of having their own way! This man's car might be 'waiting outside' for her, but she had no intention of getting into it. They were too arrogant by far, both uncle and nephew!

She gave Henry a vaguely dismissive smile before disappearing off to the staff-rooms where she had left her own clothes when she had changed earlier.

She had never been so glad to get back into her own familiar denims and black jumper neatly tucked in at her waist, brushing her hair loosely about her shoulders in a silver-blonde curtain. If Lyon Buchanan had imagined she actually liked wearing that awful bunny girl outfit . . . !

The humour of the situation suddenly hit her, and she sat down on a chair in the staff-room as she succumbed to the laughter, easily able to imagine Lyon Buchanan's apoplectic horror at finding a half-clothed woman cavorting around his store. My God, it was a wonder he hadn't been the one to have the heart attack!

That particular part of it sobered her slightly. Henry Whoever-he-was—certainly not a Buchanan if his opinion of the Buchanan family was anything to go by!—really should go and see a doctor after collapsing in that way; she agreed with Lyon Buchanan over——

It was none of her business, she firmly admonished herself. Besides, she had no wish to agree with Lyon Buchanan over anything!

The fact that she almost walked into the man himself as she came out of the staff-room did nothing to settle her already jangled nerves; the last thing she wanted was another verbal shredding from Lyon Buchanan before she could make good her escape! But as he looked at her blankly with those metallic grey eyes, she realised he hadn't even recognised her! Maybe he had taken more notice of the briefness of the bunny girl outfit than he liked to admit, after all!

But as those grey eyes suddenly narrowed in recognition, the sculpted mouth thinning, Silke knew she wasn't going to escape that easily. Damn!

He came to an abrupt halt in front of her, still towering over her now that Silke was wearing flat black ankle boots. Not that it would have made a lot of difference if she were wearing the high-heeled shoes she had had on earlier; this man was at least a foot taller than her.

'You seem shorter than I remember,' he suddenly bit out. 'Besides which, I didn't recognise you with your clothes on.'

Silke gave an involuntary gasp at the outrageousness of the remark, looking about them self-consciously, knowing by the speculative smile being exchanged by two female shoppers a short distance away that the clear timbre of Lyon's voice had reached them, at least. 'Didn't recognise you with your clothes on', indeed! She hadn't got away with the defiance of accepting his uncle's offer of a lift, against this man's obvious wishes, as lightly as she had thought she had . . . !

Her eyes flashed deeply green as she looked up at him, her hand tightly gripping the bag containing the costume that had caused her all this trouble in the first place. 'Height doesn't seem to matter when you're lying horizontal, does it?' She smiled up at him sweetly, challenge in her eyes now.

'*Touché*,' he drawled appreciatively, also aware of their audience, the two women having moved a little closer now on the pretext of looking at a rack of scarves near them, seemingly enthralled by the conversation. 'Not in the least,' Lyon spoke loudly enough for the two women to hear again now. 'Shall we arrange a time for us to lie horizontal together again?'

This conversation, as far as Silke was concerned, was getting totally out of control! And it was so unexpected from a man who, minutes ago, had seemed so icily remote that a raging fire wouldn't have melted that cold reserve. She was sure his uncle, a man who obviously knew him reasonably well, wouldn't believe the humorous—albeit at her expense!—innuendoes of the conversation. But it *was* at her expense, and there could be no doubting that Lyon Buchanan was enjoying putting her at a disadvantage.

She moved closer to him, standing on tiptoe, giving the appearance of intimacy—very aware of their listening and watching audience. 'Actually——' she spoke conspiratorially, but still loud enough for the two women to hear '—while I found our last—encounter interesting, it isn't one I want to repeat!' She looked up at Lyon Buchanan triumphantly as she saw that the two women were now looking at him with open speculation, disappointment in their faces that a man who looked so virilely handsome should—apparently!—have been such a failure in bed. 'Just my personal opinion, of course,' Silke added with feigned apology, challenge returning to her eyes as she looked up at the now stony-faced Lyon Buchanan; he certainly didn't like having the upper hand taken away from him!

His mouth was a thin line. 'And it's such an experienced opinion, isn't it?' he rasped contemptuously.

She should have known he wouldn't let her get away with that one! 'Well, one doesn't like to boast...' she returned dismissively.

He looked down at her coldly. 'In this day and age "one" would be insane to do so.'

She might be in there fighting, but she was wise enough to know she wasn't about to win in this conversation! Better to give up now, before she lost too badly... 'Well, if you'll excuse me,' she told him lightly, 'one of my other clients is waiting outside.' She gave him a falsely bright smile. 'If you should need the agency's services again, just give them a ring. But don't ask for me,' was her parting shot before she turned to give the now open-mouthed women a bright, meaningless smile on her way out of the store.

She knew exactly the impression she had given with that last comment, of herself—and Lyon Buchanan. And it was him she had meant to hit out at. She didn't particularly care for herself, knew who she was, also what she was, and the opinion of two women she was never likely to see again was completely unimportant to her. Lyon Buchanan was the one who needed to be shown that she didn't consider herself one of his underlings whom he could browbeat with his damned arrogance, or a woman he could 'frighten away' with his rudeness.

Arrogant. Self-opinionated. Chauvinistic. Silke had never met a man like him before!

And she didn't want to meet him again either.

Though there was no reason on this earth why she ever should!

'Stop laughing, Mother.' Silke frowned across at her mother as she rocked back and forth in the leather chair behind her desk. 'God!' She gave an impatient sigh. 'I was worried sick you would be upset about annoying Buchanan himself, and instead you go off into hysterical laughter! I should have realised your warped sense of humour would find the situation funny!' She sat down dejectedly in the chair opposite her mother.

Tina Jordan, an older version of Silke, sobered slightly, her mouth still twitching as she tried to contain her laughter, laughter that had convulsed her ever since Silke had told her what had happened to her after the discovery of the mistake over the rabbit outfit.

'Sorry.' She chewed on her top lip in an effort to stop herself laughing again. 'It's just that I would have loved to have seen the look on Lyon Buchanan's face when he first saw you dressed up as a bunny girl and not the fluffy bunny he had been expecting!' Green eyes, so like Silke's, glittered with suppressed humour.

'Believe me,' Silke groaned at the memory, 'you wouldn't!'

Her mother sobered slightly. 'Maybe not,' she acknowledged drily. 'Doug Moore sounded under more than a little pressure when he telephoned a short time ago.'

Remembering the grim determination on Lyon Buchanan's face as she hastily left his office, Silke thought 'more than a little pressure' was probably putting it mildly—very mildly! 'Well, I for one am not going back there, Mother,' she said firmly. 'You don't pay enough for me to put myself through clashing with Lyon Buchanan again.' She still shuddered at the thought of her disastrous morning.

'You don't have to go back,' her mother assured her with a shake of her head. 'Nadine's audition didn't go well this morning, so I've sent her along to Buchanan's.'

Silke could hardly contain her relief. And then she berated herself for being such a coward. Who was Lyon Buchanan, anyway? Just a man. An arrogantly powerful one, yes, but still just a man.

'What's he like?'

She gave her mother a sharp look. She hadn't realised she was being watched, that her every expression would give away her confused anger where Lyon Buchanan was concerned. And that would intrigue her mother—the fact that Silke had reacted to Lyon Buchanan at all. Because she hadn't reacted to any man for almost a year. Since James. The man she had been dating for three years. The man who, on the eve of their wedding, had eloped with a girl he had only met the week before!

Since that time, Silke had considered that men weren't worth bothering with, that she couldn't put her trust in any of them. Her mother had been telling her as much for years, but, like the naïve idiot she had been, Silke had thought James was different. The two of them had been friends as much as anything else, so in effect she felt she had been let down not only by the man she loved but by her friend as well.

'He's just a man, Mother,' she dismissed with a grimace, not wanting to give away the fact that he was probably unlike any other man she had ever met.

'Yes, but——' Her mother broke off the conversation as the office door opened, her smile one of polite enquiry as she turned towards what she hoped was a prospective client.

But the smile froze on her lips, and the colour faded from her cheeks, her eyes wide.

Silke frowned at this sudden change in her mother, turning towards the door herself, her frown deepening as she saw 'Uncle Henry' standing there. What on earth——?

'Hal...!' Her mother's voice was a strangulated croak.

'Satin!' Henry returned with satisfaction, grey eyes glowing excitedly.

Hal? Satin! Her mother's name was Tina, so—but what did it matter what her mother's name was, when it was perfectly obvious that Henry and her mother knew each other, and more than casually if her mother's stunned reaction was anything to go by, her mother standing up now, still very pale, and totally unable to tear her gaze away from Henry—Hal...?

And, as Silke looked at the two of them, she couldn't help wondering if it had been her likeness to her mother that had caused Henry's collapse earlier...

CHAPTER THREE

'SATIN!' Henry cried protestingly as, much to Silke's amazement, her mother pushed her chair back and rushed from the room, a hunted look on her ravished face.

And Silke *was* amazed—because, as far as she knew, her mother had never run from a situation in her life!

Or maybe, just maybe, her mother had been running all her life...?

Silke had never quite looked at her mother's unsettled life in that way before, but in retrospect, with her mother's reaction to 'Hal', perhaps there was another reason than wanderlust for her mother having travelled so much in her life in the way that she had. It——

'I knew it,' Henry gasped from across the room. 'I thought—I hoped it might be true when I first saw you, Silke, but once you had told me your name——!' He shook his head dazedly.

'Satin' and Silke...

'—I just knew it had to be true,' Henry continued wonderingly—before promptly collapsing.

For the second time that day!

But this time Silke knew exactly what to do, getting one of the pills from the bottle in his breast pocket, forcing it into his mouth, down on her haunches beside him as she waited for the pill to begin to work.

Except that this time he still looked ashen when he regained consciousness, though considering this was

39

the second attack he had had in as many hours, that wasn't surprising. Besides, this time he had fallen too, albeit on to a carpeted floor.

Silke smiled at him reassuringly as he blinked up at her dazedly. 'I'm going to call for an ambulance,' she told him gently, not wanting to alarm him further, but knowing he really should see a doctor this time.

He swallowed hard, shaking his head. 'Call Lyon,' he bit out, in obvious pain still. 'He'll know what to do.'

She didn't doubt for a moment that Lyon Buchanan would know *exactly* what to do! She also knew she shouldn't let her aversion to him influence her actions when this elderly man's health was at stake. But the very thought of seeing Lyon Buchanan again...!

'Please call Lyon.' Henry looked up at her pleadingly, grey eyes dull with pain.

'Of course I will,' Silke instantly assured him, swallowing down her own aversion to seeing that hateful man again—so much for her being sure she would never have any reason to do so! And she had her mother's strange behaviour to deal with yet, too. 'But first, do you feel well enough to move over to the chair?' she prompted encouragingly.

His eyes brightened slightly. 'Satin's chair?' he suggested hopefully.

There was that ridiculous name for her mother again... Silke really had to find out the story behind that. But not yet. Right now she had something more important to deal with. 'If that's what you want,' she nodded agreement, helping Henry to his feet, holding his arm supportively as he swayed slightly.

The look of supreme satisfaction on the face of the elderly man as he sat in the chair Silke's mother had so recently fled from—to where?—was almost painful to see, Henry relaxing back in the leather chair with a relieved sigh, his eyes closed, his thoughts goodness knew where. Silke intended finding out exactly where as soon as she could find her mother—if she hadn't done one of her flits again. And, knowing her mother as well as she did, Silke wouldn't put that past her, either!

But for the moment she put thoughts of her mother to the back of her mind, concentrating on what she had to do here and now—and that was telephone Lyon Buchanan!

The telephone number of Buchanan's was in the file on her mother's desk, the switchboard immediately putting her call through to Lyon Buchanan's secretary.

'Could I ask the reason for the call?' the woman asked warily once Silke had identified herself.

She wouldn't put it past Lyon Buchanan to have instructed his secretary to vet any calls from Jordan's Miracles! 'It's personal,' she snapped unhelpfully, feeling immediately guilty for allowing her resentment towards Lyon Buchanan to affect her response as she glanced across the room and saw how pale and haggard Henry still looked. 'I have to talk to Mr Buchanan immediately,' she added more urgently.

There was a click, a short pause—very short!—and then the arrogantly sure voice Silke recognised only too well came on the line. 'I thought we had concluded our earlier—conversation, Miss Jordan,' Lyon Buchanan drawled contemptuously.

Silke still cringed when she thought of that double-edged conversation, wishing now that she had never

engaged in such a futile verbal battle with this particular man. It had been an act of bravado on her
part, not to say childish, and it made talking to him
now all the more difficult. 'It's Henry,' she said
without preamble—she still didn't know the surname
of the elderly man, and at the moment he didn't look
capable of telling it to her. 'He's collapsed again,
and——'

'My God,' Lyon Buchanan exploded. 'What have
you done to him now?'

Her cheeks burned with indignation. 'I haven't done
anything to him!' Henry was actually asleep at the
moment. 'He——'

'Where are you?' Lyon Buchanan interrupted
harshly.

'At the agency. But——'

'I'm on my way,' he told her coldly. 'Just don't do
anything else to him before I get there!' He slammed
his receiver down, the noise resounding in Silke's ear.

Silke slammed her own receiver down too—and then
glanced guiltily at Henry. But he continued to sleep—
thank goodness.

Just what did the Lyon think she had 'done' to his
uncle? Remembering the conversation they had had
earlier, she could make a pretty accurate guess. My
God, the arrogance of the man; did he really think
that because she had denied being an out-of-work ac-
tress her other line of business had to be...? He did
think that, she was sure of it from his tone of voice
just now. He probably believed his uncle had collapsed again because they had been—— Arrogant, arrogant swine!

She could not remember ever feeling this angry in
her life before, not even once she had got over the

initial pain of James's defection on the eve of their wedding. And it was an anger that didn't lessen as the time ticked by!

'You look just like your mother when you're angry, my dear.'

Silke looked sharply across the room at Henry, a blush darkening her cheeks now as she realised he had woken up and had obviously been watching her for some time.

She drew in a deeply controlling breath. 'I probably feel like her when I'm angry too!' she told him with feeling.

'Lyon has that effect on people,' he nodded, sobering slightly, a little colour having returned to his cheeks after his ten-minute nap. 'I remember I used to make your mother angry a lot,' he said heavily. 'Do you think she'll come back?' He looked longingly towards the door where her mother had so recently fled.

Silke sighed as she moved to his side, offering no objection as he lightly clasped her hand as he had the last time. 'I'm really not sure,' she answered him honestly. 'My mother has always been a law unto herself.' She grimaced as she remembered the chaotic years of her early childhood, when she had never been quite sure what her mother might do.

Henry gave a half-smile. 'I remember that too,' he nodded.

Despite the fact that she realised how ill this man was, Silke's curiosity momentarily got the better of her. 'How——?' She broke off abruptly as the office door burst open without warning, her initial hope that it might be her mother immediately dashed as Lyon Buchanan strode purposefully into the room.

He came to an abrupt halt just inside the door, taking in the scene with one cold glance, his narrowed gaze raking scathingly over Silke's hand so cosily enfolded in his uncle's much larger one.

Silke's initial reaction was to pull her hand sharply away, but at the first sign that she was about to do that Henry's hand tightened its grip. She looked down at him, knowing by his determined expression that he wasn't about to release her without a fuss. And that she could do without!

Instead she turned her frustrated anger on Lyon Buchanan—he was the reason for it anyway! 'What did you do?' she said scathingly. 'Fly here?' She returned his gaze as challengingly as he was now looking at her.

'Almost,' he bit out grimly, his attention turning to his uncle, although the older man was obviously slightly recovered now. 'When are you going to realise you're nearly seventy years old?' Lyon said impatiently.

'Sixty-seven, boy,' his uncle returned with some of his earlier spirit. 'And don't worry, I've just decided I'm going to be around for a lot more years yet.' His softened gaze rested on Silke after he had made this statement.

Lyon Buchanan's hard gaze returned to her too, a sharp questioning in those icy eyes as he took in the blush that seemed to be becoming a permanent fixture in Silke's usually creamy cheeks. 'Indeed?' he finally bit out tersely. 'Well, I think we should get you to Peter Carruthers and let him decide that, don't you?' he said scathingly. 'Can you walk, or shall I——?'

'I can walk,' his uncle assured him firmly. 'And I want Silke to come with me.'

Now it was Silke's turn to look at him sharply. She was worried about him herself, and, much as she would have hated having to contact Lyon Buchanan again, she had intended telephoning him later to assure herself that his uncle was indeed OK. But she hadn't considered actually going along with Henry to see his doctor!

'Now that I've found you, I'm not going to let you out of my sight again until we've talked further. I'm sure you can guess why,' Henry told her ruefully.

Because of her mother. 'Satin' had run away, but he had no intention of letting her daughter escape as easily. And if Silke was honest she was more than a little curious to know more about 'Hal' and 'Satin' herself!

But she could see from Lyon Buchanan's furious expression, and the angry glitter in his eyes, that he had completely misread the situation—and that he didn't like his conclusions one little bit! Well, Silke didn't give a damn how he felt about it; she would accompany Henry!

'Of course I'll come with you.' She squeezed the elderly man's hand reassuringly. No matter how much Lyon Buchanan might hate it!

And as they helped Henry out of the office and down to Lyon Buchanan's car—parked illegally on double yellow lines; what else?—it was obvious how much he did hate Silke's presence there, his eyes glittering down coldly at her as they stood either side of Henry to help him down the stairs and out into the street. And his face was set in grimly disapproving lines as Henry insisted he wanted Silke to sit beside him in the back of the silver Mercedes.

'You'll have more room to make yourself comfortable if Miss Jordan sits in the front next to me,' he told his uncle harshly, somehow managing to infuse a wealth of contempt into the 'Miss Jordan'.

Making Silke feel like kicking him up the seat of his tailored trousers! In fact, the temptation was so strong that she had to turn her attention firmly to Henry to actually stop herself carrying out the action. 'I think, in this case, your nephew is probably right,' she told the elderly man gently, seeing an answering humour in Henry's eyes as his lips twitched in appreciation of her insertion of 'in this case'. But, as far as she was concerned, Lyon Buchanan was wrong about most other things; he was a man who made assumptions and then acted upon them. 'It isn't far, is it?' she prompted the arrogant man as she climbed into the passenger seat, concerned at how white Henry now looked as he slumped down in the back seat.

'Not too far,' Lyon replied tersely, slamming her car door closed to stride purposefully around to the driver's side of the powerful vehicle.

There was a husky chuckle from the back seat. 'I haven't seen him this angry in years,' Henry mused softly.

She turned to look at him. 'That's probably because he's been surrounded by "yes-men"—and women!—for years!' She scowled.

Henry raised grey brows. 'There's no danger of that from you, is there?' he said with satisfaction.

'None at all,' she assured him firmly, turning back in her seat as Lyon climbed in beside her.

There was an instant tension in the interior of the car that hadn't been there seconds earlier; the very air seemed charged with the electricity of resentment that flowed between Silke and Lyon. His expression was grim as he manoeuvred the car out into the flow of traffic, his mouth set in disapproving lines, dark brows frowning over those icy grey eyes.

And then Silke noticed his hands. They were long and slender, almost artistic-looking. Even the fact that the nails were kept cut practically short couldn't detract from the fact that Lyon Buchanan's hands were long and tapered—and beautiful.

Silke looked quickly away as she realised how ridiculous her thoughts had been, a blush to her cheeks. There was *nothing* beautiful about Lyon Buchanan. He was arrogant. And cold. Contemptuous of his fellow man—and woman. *Especially* woman, from her own experience with him. It couldn't be her personally that he disliked; he didn't even know her.

She didn't know him either, but then she didn't want to!

She just wouldn't look at his hands again . . .

'Could you check to see if he's just fallen asleep or if he's had another attack?' Lyon spoke abruptly at her side, startling her.

She turned quickly to look at Henry. The elderly man was slumped right down on the back seat now, his eyes closed. With a slight adjustment of her seatbelt she was able to reach far enough back to check the pulse at Henry's wrist. It was steady and strong. 'He's asleep,' she replied, with some relief, as she turned back in her seat.

Lyon's cold grey gaze raked over her briefly before his attention returned to negotiating the traffic. 'You do realise I shall want a full explanation from you about what happened,' he bit out harshly.

Silke gasped indignantly at the accusation in his voice. 'I told you——'

'Not now,' he told her grimly. 'I want to make sure Henry is going to be all right first.'

Before he verbally ripped her to shreds! He hadn't actually said that, but the implication was definitely there in his voice.

Silke's mouth firmed with stubborn determination as she stared straight ahead during the rest of the drive. She would stay only long enough to make sure Henry was going to be all right too—and then she was leaving! Without talking to Lyon Buchanan. She had nothing to 'explain'!

Peter Carruthers' clinic was exactly that sort of private place she would have expected Lyon Buchanan to take his uncle—expensive, too, Silke would guess from its appearance. And just the appearance of the arrogant millionaire was enough to make the staff jump into action. Peter Carruthers himself was with Henry in the short few minutes it took for one of the nurses to tell him of their arrival.

Silke took herself off to the plush waiting-room, feeling completely superfluous as Lyon Buchanan accompanied his uncle for the examination without giving her a backward glance. But she couldn't disappear completely—much as she would like to—without first making sure Henry was going to recover fully.

Even the waiting-room reflected the wealth of the people who obviously visited this clinic: fresh coffee percolating on the side, bone-china cups, a jug of fresh cream set on the table beside it. Even the magazines on the low table in front of the comfortable leather armchairs were current issues—unlike the ancient ones usually found in clinics and hospital waiting-rooms.

As Silke helped herself to some of the aromatic coffee she decided it was probably the least comfort the consultant could provide for the exuberant fees he no doubt charged his patients!

To her dismay Lyon Buchanan entered the room just as she was sitting down with her coffee, and some of the hot brew spilled over into the china saucer as she looked up and saw him. Surely Henry hadn't been examined already...?

'Peter can do his job better without me present,' Lyon Buchanan informed her tersely as he helped himself to the coffee.

Silke could have done her waiting better alone too— but obviously she didn't have the same authority to request it as the consultant had!

She eyed Lyon warily as he poured his coffee, not in the least surprised when he shunned both the cream and sugar—both of which she had helped herself to a liberal amount of seconds ago! Obviously Lyon didn't have the same sweet tooth she did. In fact, if she was honest, she had probably eaten more of those free chocolate bunnies herself this morning than she had actually given away!

She could feel her tension rising as, after pouring the coffee, he moved across the room to sit down, sipping the steaming hot brew, all without saying a word. And in the circumstances her tension was ridiculous; she had nothing to feel in the least guilty about where this man was concerned. Except wear the wrong bunny outfit to work in his store, and she didn't consider that her fault either!

'How is Henry?' She decided to take the initiative as the silence became more and more fraught with tension—on her part!—the longer it went on. 'I'm sorry, I still don't know his surname,' she added awkwardly as dark brows rose over icy grey eyes.

Lyon's mouth thinned even more at the admission. 'You didn't get as far as exchanging last names?' His contempt was obvious.

Her eyes flashed angrily at his implication. For God's sake, Henry was old enough to be her grandfather!

'It's Winter,' Lyon supplied abruptly. 'Obviously Peter is going to do the appropriate tests, but he seems to think Henry will be fine after a few days in bed.'

Silke was relieved; she had become quite fond of the elderly man in the short time she had known him. And, if what she suspected about Henry and her mother was true, then her mother had once been more than fond of him!

'Alone,' Lyon added harshly before she could make any response.

Her eyes widened with indignation. 'Now look——'

'I told you before—I have,' he drawled hardly, leaning forward to put his empty cup down on the table, his scathing gaze never leaving her angrily flushed face.

'And I don't meet your "requirements",' Silke recalled dismissively.

He gave an acknowledging inclination of his head. 'But obviously you meet my uncle's,' he said disgustedly.

She shook her head at the arrogant assumption of this man. She had never met anyone quite like him before! 'Do you think this badly of everyone you meet, Mr Buchanan?' she challenged scornfully. 'Or am I just the lucky one?'

The look he gave her was scathing in the extreme. 'Women like you make me——'

' "Women like me"?' This time her indignation got the better of her as she sat ramrod-straight in the edge of her chair.

'—sick,' he finished disgustedly, as if she hadn't just interrupted him, standing up as he did so, immediately dominating the room with his superior height. Although this man didn't need his height, or his muscular build, to achieve that; he had an aura of power that would be apparent no matter what he looked like. 'What on earth do you think you're doing with a man as old as Henry?' He stood over her now, his close proximity threatening, his expression coldly furious.

'I——'

'Lyon, do you think we could talk now?' interrupted the quietly authoritative voice of Peter Carruthers.

Lyon turned sharply to face the other man, and as Silke turned to look at him too, his expression innocently enquiring, she couldn't help wondering how much of their conversation he had actually overheard before interrupting them; their voices hadn't exactly been discreetly lowered! And as the consultant looked at her speculatively, Silke knew he had overheard far too much for her to feel comfortable remaining here any longer!

She stood up decisively. 'I think I'll leave now. As long as Hen—Mr Winter is going to be all right?' Now that she knew the elderly man's surname it sounded

inappropriate—to her at least!—to call him by anything else. She could feel Lyon Buchanan's contemptuous gaze upon her, but she ignored that in
favour of looking at Peter Carruthers for his answer.

The consultant gave her a politely reassuring smile.
'He's going to be fine,' he nodded non-committally.

That was good enough for Silke. She had done her
bit as far as she was concerned, had accompanied
Henry here as he had wanted her to; she had no intention of hanging around to listen to more of Lyon
Buchanan's insults! 'I'll telephone later and check on
his condition, if that's OK,' she told Peter Carruthers,
totally ignoring the brooding figure of Lyon
Buchanan; she felt as if, if she looked at him again,
she might give in to that impulse she had had earlier
to kick him anywhere she could reach!

'Of course,' the consultant returned smoothly. 'And
your name is?'

Of course, the staff at this clinic wouldn't give out
information on one of the patients here to just anyone.
'Silke Jordan,' she supplied stiltedly, still ignoring
Lyon Buchanan's gaze, but easily able to guess at the
contempt she would see in his face towards her if she
should chance a glance at him; the damned man never
seemed to look at her in any other way!

But, with the opinion he had of her relationship
with his uncle, that wasn't surprising. How she would
love to wipe that superior smile off his face—the only
problem was, she never would, because he was never
going to believe anything she told him.

'Miss Jordan,' Peter Carruthers answered her.
'We'll expect your call,' he nodded.

Feeling dismissed, Silke headed towards the door.
If she were honest—and she wished she needn't be!—

she had to stop herself from breaking into a run, so anxious was she to get away from Lyon Buchanan.

'Silke.'

Softly spoken in that way, her name on Lyon Buchanan's lips nevertheless carried a wealth of authority. An authority Silke would have loved to ignore—and yet knew that she couldn't, not with the other man present. She turned as she reached the door, her hand already on the handle, straightening even more defensively as she saw Lyon's gaze fall mockingly on the movement. She returned his gaze enquiringly, the silence stretching awkwardly between them as he kept her waiting for his next statement.

'I'll be in touch,' he finally told her quietly.

She didn't doubt it—but he would have to find her first. She didn't actually work for her mother's agency, only filled in if her mother was desperate, like today, and once she had spoken to her mother—if she could find her!—she would make sure her mother didn't give this man her address. This time she had no intention of ever seeing this hateful man, with his nasty suspicious mind, ever again!

She nodded distantly. 'My mother will be pleased to take your call.' Although if her mother's reaction to Henry Winter was anything to go by, Silke doubted her mother would be any more thrilled to hear from a member of this family than she would!

Dark brows rose over grey eyes. 'Your mother?'

Silke could have kicked herself; he obviously hadn't made the connection—despite her name—between herself and the owner of Jordan's Miracles.

'Your business is with her agency,' Silke supplied coldly. 'She'll be happy to deal with you,' she lied, sure that once her mother learned of Henry Winter's connection to Buchanan's she would sever the contract with them, no matter how important she had considered it earlier this morning.

Lyon Buchanan's mouth tightened ominously. 'Your mother owns the agency, and yet she sent you out this morning looking like a——'

'I believe an apology has already been made for that particular mistake,' Silke snapped abruptly, very aware of Peter Carruthers' silent interest in their conversation—and she didn't want the whole world to know of her involvement over the fiasco of her bunny girl outfit. 'I'll call later to check on Mr Winter,' she told the consultant now, determined to make good her escape this time.

'You haven't heard the last of me, Silke,' Lyon Buchanan told her harshly.

This time Silke left without even acknowledging his remark. He was obviously a man who wanted—and was accustomed to having!—the last word. Let him have it, if he needed it that badly; she just wanted to leave.

She was trembling by the time she emerged from the clinic, realising she was more shaken by their conversation than she wanted to admit. But, she consoled herself, she doubted she would be the first person—or indeed the last!—to find him so intimidating. It just irked her that he had had that effect on her. After James she had sworn no man would ever unsettle her, or her life, ever again. Lyon Buchanan more than unsettled her; he angered her to the point of making her want to scream!

She wasn't in the least surprised to find the office locked, and neither Jackie, her mother's secretary, nor her mother actually present when Silke finally got back to the agency just after five o'clock. In fact, she doubted her mother had returned at all today; Jackie had probably been the one to lock up before going home herself. Silke would be surprised if she actually found her mother at her elegant apartment either; from her childhood memories of her mother, when she wanted to leave, she just went.

Silke's heart sank—and she felt like leaving herself when she emerged from the building that housed her mother's agency to find an all too familiar silver Mercedes screeching to a halt beside the pavement, a furious-looking Lyon Buchanan climbing jerkily out from behind the wheel, the violent slamming of the car door behind him evidence that his mood hadn't improved from earlier—in fact, from the glittering fury in his eyes as he spotted her, it had got worse! What on earth had she done now? Silke wondered warily.

He towered over her ominously as he came to an abrupt halt in front of her, a nerve pulsing in his cheek the only sign that he wasn't as in control as he usually appeared to be.

'You're a fast worker, I'll give you that,' he ground out between clenched teeth, the nerve in his cheek pulsing even more erratically.

Silke blinked up at him frowningly. 'Sorry?'

'Not as sorry as you're going to be,' he assured her hardly, the lean fingers of one hand tightly grasping the top or her arm as he began to march her towards his car.

This man was far too fond of frog-marching and bullying her into going places she didn't want to go, and quite frankly Silke had had enough of it. More than enough!

She wrenched out of his grasp, wincing at the pain this caused to exactly the same bruised spot where he had grasped her earlier. She was going to be very badly bruised by the time he had finished with her. Or she had finished with him, which she was just about to do!

'I don't know what your problem is now, Mr Buchanan,' she told him heatedly. 'And, quite frankly, I have no wish to know either! Just as I have no wish to be manhandled by you again——'

'Think yourself lucky it's only your arm I've hurt,' he rasped as she rubbed the bruised spot. 'What I would really like to do is wring your damned neck!' He glared down at her.

Considering they were standing in the middle of a busy street, office workers pouring out of the building on either side of them, pushing past the two of them in their rush to get home, it might be a little difficult for him to actually carry out that particular threat at the moment. Although, knowing him as she did, Silke wasn't so sure of that...

What on earth had she done now?

'My uncle,' he bit out viciously, 'has just informed me that he's met the woman he intends making his wife!'

Silke looked up at him blankly. But, as Lyon continued to glare down at her, realisation began to dawn!

'Don't look so innocent, Silke,' Lyon rasped savagely. 'You know damn well I'm talking about you. Henry has just informed me that he intends marrying you as soon as he can persuade you to say yes!' His coldly contemptuous gaze raked over her. 'Which I'm sure won't take him too long!'

Silke couldn't speak, couldn't have uttered a word if she had tried. What was the man talking about?

CHAPTER FOUR

LYON BUCHANAN'S mouth twisted derisively as Silke continued to gape up at him. 'Don't try and tell me the news has come as a surprise to you,' he snapped contemptuously. 'You must have done something to encourage Henry to think along those lines.'

She shook her head dazedly. 'I don't know what you're talking about.'

'No?' Lyon said scathingly. 'Henry has lived for sixty-seven years without contemplating marriage to any woman, and yet after meeting you this morning he suddenly decides to take the plunge; forgive me, Silke, if I find your shock a little hard to believe!'

She was starting to come out of the shock now, and as she did, she knew that Lyon had made an error of some sort. Most unusual for him, she was sure! But she had seen the way Henry looked at her mother earlier, her mother's reaction to seeing him, knew that there had once been—possibly still was, if her mother's flight at the mere sight of Henry was any-thing to go by!—some very strong emotion between the older couple. In fact . . .

'What exactly did your uncle say?' she prompted guardedly.

Lyon's nostrils flared angrily. 'I told you——'

'I said *exactly*,' Silke reminded him quietly, her mind racing.

He drew in a harsh breath. 'Henry was slightly groggy by the time I managed to talk to him; Peter had given him something to help him relax. But Henry made a point of telling me he was going to marry you as soon as he's out of hospital,' his voice rose angrily again over the last.

'Not me,' Silke told him firmly, frowning, positive now Henry hadn't been talking about her. Just what sort of relationship had Henry and her mother had in the past for Henry to have made such a statement to his nephew?

'Of course it was you, damn it!' Lyon looked as if he were about to explode. 'You——'

'Satin,' Silke said with certainty, preoccupied with thoughts of her mother and Henry. 'I'm sure Henry told you he was going to marry Satin.' She looked at him enquiringly.

'Silke, Satin, it's the same thing; I told you, he was groggy when I spoke to him,' Lyon dismissed impatiently.

Not too groggy to know exactly who he was talking about—and what he wanted! My God, her mother had some explaining to do!

'You're wrong, Mr Buchanan,' Silke shook her head ruefully. 'It isn't the same thing at all. And I'm sure when your uncle feels less—groggy he'll tell you that himself.'

'And I'm telling you that I have no intention of letting a little gold-digger like you marry my uncle!' he bit out contemptuously.

Silke frowned up at him. He really was the most insulting——! 'And just exactly what right do you think you have to tell anyone who they should or shouldn't marry?' she scorned. 'From the little I've seen of you, you wouldn't know love if it jumped up and bit you on the nose!' She was breathing hard in her agitation. What right did he have to call her a gold-digger? He didn't even know her. Or her mother. Which, if she wasn't mistaken, was going to be more to the point—because she was sure it was her mother Henry had decided he was going to marry. And she was no more a gold-digger than Silke was.

Lyon's face might have been carved out of granite, his mouth a thin, angry line. 'You aren't trying to tell me you love my uncle?' he derided harshly.

'Not yet,' she answered vaguely. But if what she suspected were to become fact, she had a feeling she was going to be put in a position where she could possibly learn to love him as a stepfather. If Henry ever persuaded her mother to stop running. And Silke was positive he was going to have a damn good try at doing exactly that!

'But you might be able to force yourself,' Lyon rasped with contempt. 'Taking into account his bank balance—and his obvious ill-health. After all, the chances are, with his heart complaint, that you wouldn't have to be married to him for too long before he——'

Silke had never hit anyone in her life before. Until that moment. And there was no thought behind it now either, just an instinctive response to the insult Lyon was making to both her and Henry. Just who did this man think he was? How dared he say those things about her after knowing her for so brief a time?

But if she thought she was angry then, her emotions were mild in comparison with his; his face was deathly white, a nerve pulsing in one rigidly clenched cheek, the red marks where her fingers had made contact standing out lividly against that abnormal paleness.

But as usual it was his eyes that were most expressive, glittering dangerously, almost silver in their intensity.

Silke stared up at him wordlessly, shocked by her own actions as much as by his reaction to it.

'You're going to regret you ever did that,' he finally ground out between clenched, perfectly even white teeth.

She didn't doubt it, had realised that the moment her hand made contact with that hard cheek! But there was no way she was going to stand by and let this man insult her—and his uncle!—in the way he had been doing.

'Goodbye, Mr Buchanan,' she told him with as much dignity as she could muster, turning away to join the milling crowd, people that had only been momentarily diverted in their hurry to get home by the scene taking place on the pavement between the tall, autocratic man and the slender, blonde-haired young woman.

As she walked away, Silke half expected those steely fingers to grasp her once again. But as she took each step further away from Lyon Buchanan and it didn't happen, she began to breathe again, resisting the impulse to turn and look back at him to see exactly what he had done after she walked away, whether he had gone back to his car or was still standing on the pavement where she had left him. No doubt he had roared off in the other direction in his powerful car, thoughts of revenge already forming in his calculating mind!

Silke realised she was trembling with reaction. God, that man was—well, he just *was*! She had never met anyone like him before. And she hoped she never did again!

*   *   *

Her mother hadn't, as it turned out, run very far. Silke knew, by the lights blazing in her mother's apartment as she approached the prestigious building, that her mother was definitely at home. It was something, at least.

The fact that her mother was in the kitchen baking bread wasn't a good sign; it was her mother's other escape. All through her haphazard childhood Silke could remember the smell of baking bread whenever her mother had hit another disaster in her life—and there had been many!

It was obvious, from the slightly red-rimmed green eyes as their gazes met across the kitchen, that her mother had been crying. A lot, from her make-up-less cheeks; her mother was always perfectly groomed and made-up.

She abruptly broke off her fierce pummelling of the dough to frown at the distress clearly written on Silke's pale face. 'What happened?' she asked heavily.

Too much for her to be able to tell it all! She couldn't believe it was only just over eight hours since she had gone, under protest, to take up her position in the confectionery department of Buchanan's; it seemed as if a lifetime had passed since Lyon Buchanan had verbally ripped into her before dragging her up to his office.

But Lyon Buchanan wouldn't be where her mother's interest lay...

'Henry Winter collapsed after you ran out of the office this after—steady!' Silke warned concernedly as her mother swayed slightly, her face going even paler.

Silke hurried to pull out a chair from the kitchen table, sitting her mother down in it before moving to sit in the chair opposite, looking across at her worriedly; there could be no doubting her mother's distress at the news.

Her mother moistened dry lips. 'Is he—is he——?'

'He's in a private clinic,' Silke reassured gently. She had never seen her mother shaken like this; there must have been something very special between her mother and Henry Winter for her to be reacting like this. 'I'm going to telephone later to see if he's——'

'Just tell me where it is.' Her mother stood up abruptly, already taking off her apron before moving to wash her flour-covered hands.

Silke frowned at her. 'But a short time ago you ran away from the man——'

'Just tell me, Silke,' her mother repeated sharply, her face more pale and strained than ever. 'Today wasn't the first time I ran away from Hal,' she added stiltedly. 'I think, this time—in the circumstances—I owe him an explanation.' She looked pained at the thought.

Silke had guessed some of what might have occurred between the older couple in the past, and 'in the circumstances' maybe it would be fairer to Henry Winter not to tell her mother he wasn't in any immediate danger; she knew too well herself how far and how ably her mother could run when she set her mind to it. Henry would never find her!

So instead she told her mother exactly where the clinic was, assuring her she would clear away the mess she had been making when Silke arrived.

'But if you run into the nephew—beware!' she thought it prudent to advise her mother as she left, remembering all too clearly her own run-ins with Lyon Buchanan. 'He's very protective of his uncle,' she added by way of explanation—although she knew that wasn't strictly the truth; Lyon Buchanan had an arrogant disdain about him that owed nothing to family loyalty.

'So he damn well should be,' her mother replied scathingly. 'I'll call you if I'm going to be late,' she added dismissively.

Silke looked after her mother frowningly; just what had she meant by that parting comment concerning Lyon Buchanan? No doubt her mother would tell her soon enough, and in her own time, if she chose to, as she always had.

One thing Silke did know—Lyon Buchanan wasn't going to like it that a member of her family—Satin, no less!—was visiting his uncle...!

It was a long evening for Silke, sitting alone in the flat, wondering exactly what her mother was doing at the clinic all this time. Obviously the older couple had found a lot to talk about, but, even so, she wouldn't have thought Henry was in any condition to discuss anything too emotional.

When her mother still hadn't returned by the next morning Silke went into the agency and opened up for the day, leaving the secretary to deal with things while she went to the clinic herself, her curiosity getting the better of her now. And if anything had happened to Henry, from her mother's reaction to seeing him again after all these years, Silke didn't like to think what condition her mother was going to be in.

'Your mother is in Mr Winter's room, Miss Jordan,' the receptionist told her in answer to her query. 'Down the corridor, first door on the left,' she directed with a smile.

Silke had only to step into the room, see the truckle-bed set up in one corner as close as possible to the hospital bed where Henry lay, to know exactly where her mother had spent the night. In fact, her mother now sat in a chair beside Henry's bed, her hand firmly clasped in the elderly man's, a look of such utter contentment on both their faces as they gazed at each other that it told its own story; whatever differences this couple had had in the past, they were now very definitely behind them. Lyon Buchanan was going to be incensed all over again. If he had ever calmed down!

'Silke!' Her mother turned to her with a glowing smile. 'Darling, I'm sorry I didn't ring you last night, but——'

'It's perfectly all right, Mother,' she assured her with a smile of her own. 'From the look of you, you had other things on your mind. Hello, Henry.' She turned to the relaxed man lying in the bed, relieved to see how much better he looked. 'How are you?'

'As soon as they discharge me from here, well on my way to becoming your stepfather,' he told her wryly, that twinkle back in his eyes.

'Hal!' her mother gasped, a becoming blush heating her cheeks as she looked awkwardly across at Silke.

'We agreed that we've already wasted enough years,' her fiancé told her sternly. 'I want you to make all the arrangements so that the ceremony can take place as soon as I leave here. How do you feel about that, Silke?'

He looked almost as arrogant as his nephew at that moment. But only almost—no one could be quite as arrogant as Lyon Buchanan, in Silke's opinion! Although it gave her a glimpse of what Henry must have been like as a younger man. It made her doubly curious as to how her mother could have managed to run away from him in the first place.

'I feel fine about it,' Silke told him with a shrug.

'I've told your mother about my shocking behaviour towards you yesterday.' Henry looked a little shame-faced.

Silke nodded, crossing the room to join them. 'Warned her she'll be marrying a lecher, have you?' she teased lightly, knowing that her mother was strong enough to curb any such tendencies. And Henry had only been having a little fun, after all—albeit at her expense!

He gave a rueful grin. 'All that's going to change now I have your mother back in my life,' he assured.

Silke laughed softly. 'I'm sure it is,' she said with certainty. 'And while *I* might think it's wonderful that you've sorted out your differences and decided to get married, I know someone else who won't be so happy about it.' She raised pointed brows at Henry.

'Lyon!' he said with feeling.

'Exactly.' She grimaced.

Henry's mouth tightened determinedly. 'I'll deal with Lyon,' he told them forcefully.

After Lyon's reaction yesterday to believing Silke was the one who was about to marry his uncle, she didn't think he would be any more enamoured of the idea of her mother doing so. But if Henry thought he could 'deal' with him ... She just hoped her mother didn't get mown down in the crossfire!

'We'll deal with him together,' her mother spoke up firmly, the determined glitter in her eyes immediately dispelling any doubts Silke might have had about her mother's being able to stand up to Lyon—her mother looked like a Sherman tank about to do battle with the enemy!

In fact, her mother's next words confirmed that that was exactly how she felt about it. 'After all, he's only a Buchanan,' she said hardly.

Again there was that edge to her mother's voice when talking about Lyon Buchanan, and Silke couldn't help wondering if he had somehow been involved in the past break-up of the older couple. Although Silke didn't remember Henry Winter being one of the men her mother had been involved with when she was with her as a child, and, if her mother's and Henry's relationship had been before Silke was even born, then Lyon would only have been a child himself, surely making it unlikely that he could have any serious effect on two adults? No doubt she would get the full story from her mother—when she could manage to drag herself away from Henry's side!— and until then Silke knew she would just have to be patient where her own curiosity was concerned.

She straightened. 'I'll get back to the agency,' she told her mother, smiling affectionately as her mother reluctantly made to rise. 'I think you can take one day off, Mummy; after all, it isn't every day you become engaged!' And she had never seen her mother look so happy.

Her mother was even blushing like a schoolgirl as she stood up to hug Silke. 'I'll explain it all to you later, darling. I promise.'

As Silke went back to the office she knew it wasn't her the other couple should feel apprehensive about explaining things to, that Lyon was going to be the one they should be wary of, despite Henry's determination where his nephew was concerned.

It also dawned on her—horrifically!—that there was no longer any chance of her never seeing Lyon again, that once her mother married Henry Lyon would somehow be related to her. What a dreadful prospect!

'There's someone waiting in the office to see you,' the agency secretary told Silke as soon as she walked in through the doorway.

'Someone to see——' Silke broke off her puzzled question as she guessed from Jackie's flustered expression exactly who her visitor was; who else would be arrogant enough to demand admission to her mother's private office! 'Lyon Buchanan!' she said with feeling.

Jackie looked even more agitated. 'I don't know who he is, he didn't deign to give a name, but he's arrogant as Old Nick! I told him you wouldn't be back until later, but he insisted on waiting for you. I——'

'Don't worry about it, Jackie,' Silke soothed distractedly, glancing towards the closed inner office door, behind which she was sure Lyon Buchanan lay—sat—in wait for her. 'I quite understand your dilemma; Old Nick has nothing on this man!' She paused near the inner office door. 'And if one or both of us isn't out of this office in five minutes, then I want you to call the police—because we're probably murdering each other! Only joking, Jackie,' she assured with a rueful smile as the other girl looked more worried than ever. 'As far as I'm aware, he isn't physically violent.' It wasn't necessary when you were verbally capable of demolishing someone!

He wasn't sitting at all when Silke entered the office, but standing in front of the window, the weak March sunlight behind him clearly outlining the powerful strength of his body, the darkness of his hair taking on a silvery sheen, his hands—those hands she had to avoid looking at because their beauty totally belied the arrogant hardness of the rest of this man—thrust into the pockets of his tailored trousers. Thank God!

As he stepped forward out of the sunlight his face was thrown into sharp profile, those grey eyes taking on a silver intensity. Silke had no idea why he had returned so quickly after their heated exchange yesterday, but he certainly didn't look as if he was about to offer her an apology for his behaviour!

In fact, his next words confirmed it. 'So you've finally managed to drag yourself away from my uncle's side?' he taunted.

Silke drew in a long, controlling breath; instantly losing her temper with this man wasn't going to help the situation. If only he didn't have the ability to make her do that so easily! 'Mr Buchanan,' she greeted calmly, closing the door firmly behind her, relieved that she was at least dressed in a businesslike way this morning, her black suit complemented by an emerald-green blouse that made her eyes appear greener than ever, her hair a silky blonde cloud down past her shoulders. 'What can I do for you this morning?' She pointedly took her seat behind her mother's desk, forcing him to move away from the window to the other side of the desk if he wanted to look at her while they talked.

His mouth twisted at her brisk, businesslike tone. 'It's not what you can do for me, but what I can do for you,' he misquoted drily.

Silke quirked blonde brows enquiringly. What was the man talking about now?

He sat on the side of the desk, bringing him dangerously close to Silke, his hands out of his pockets now—a fact Silke took care to avoid looking at. 'How much do you want, Silke?'

She frowned. 'You'll receive the agency account when the bills go out at the end of the month——'

'I'm talking about you, Silke,' he cut in harshly. 'How much do you want to get out of my uncle's life?'

Maybe her joking advice to Jackie about calling the police wasn't such a joke after all; Silke felt like doing Lyon a physical injury at that moment! How dared he offer her money in that way? My God, arrogance didn't even begin to describe this man!

'Don't look so outraged,' he drawled tauntingly. 'This way you get the money but no aged husband.'

Silke was shaking so badly at this further insult from this man that she had to grip the edge of the desk so that he shouldn't see the visible trembling of her hands. No doubt Henry was right, and Lyon's own experiences with women pursuing his wealth rather than him had tempered his own outlook on life, but it didn't give him the right to judge her by those other women's standards.

'Name your price, Silke—and then we'll negotiate something a little more reasonable,' he ground out forcefully, looking down at her coldly.

She swallowed hard, breathing deeply. 'You couldn't afford me, Mr Buchanan——'

'*I* don't want you!' He stood up abruptly, moving sharply away from the desk.

Silke looked at him frowningly, at the nerve pulsing in his cheek, his tightly clenched jaw. 'Don't you?' she finally said slowly, knowing even as she said it that he *did* want her, that Lyon was physically attracted to her himself!

It was there in the angry flare in his eyes, the thinning of his tautly held mouth, the way his hands were clenched at his sides. She had thought him cold and arrogant, but she could suddenly see a raw, pulsating passion in the dark grey of his eyes. He didn't *want* to want her, but he most certainly did!

'You little——!' He moved too fast for her, Silke being still dazed by her own realisation, and before she could even offer a word of protest he had pulled her up out of her chair and into the hardness of his arms, his mouth coming down on hers with forceful intensity.

Maybe the physical attraction had been there between them from the moment they met, burning just below the surface of their antagonism, but the moment their mouths fused together it was like Guy Fawkes Night and the Fourth of July all rolled into one, sensations coursing through Silke like she had never known before, every part of her feeling alive, singing with heated desire.

Lyon's mouth moved against hers savagely, leaving no room for anything but response, Silke clinging to the broad width of his shoulders, revelling in his hands roaming restlessly across her back as he moulded her body to the lean length of his, her breasts crushed against his chest, her nipples taut and thrusting with urgent need.

And then his hands—those incredible hands; she could picture how they would look against her back, and she quivered at their lean strength against her—those hands gentled to a caress, moving beneath her jacket to touch her through the silky material of her blouse, his mouth becoming less savage, moving slowly against hers now, the tip of his tongue lightly caressing their softness before dipping inside the moistness of her mouth.

Silke felt as if her senses had been invaded: feel, taste, touch, Lyon's body feeling hard and demanding against her, the tautness of his hips provoking an excitement within her she could barely contain. And as one of those hands touched the sensitive tip of her breast she could only gasp in wonder. Lyon took advantage of her fully parted lips to thrust his tongue further into the warm cavern of her mouth, possessing her fully.

She knew that if Lyon hadn't been holding her so tightly she would have fallen to the carpeted floor at his feet, her legs feeling shaky, her body hot, engulfed in flame, her hands clinging to the broad width of his shoulders. She wanted him as much as he wanted her!

It was impossible to believe! She had met this man only yesterday, had felt antagonism towards him from the first, hadn't so much as looked at another man since James had let her down so badly, and now this——! Lyon Buchanan, of all people. She didn't want to want this man either!

'What——?' Lyon looked slightly dazed as Silke pulled abruptly away from him. 'Silke...?' He frowned down at her darkly.

She backed away from him, her eyes deep green pools of pain, her hands clasped tightly behind her back so that he couldn't see their trembling. This man already had a power over her she wouldn't have believed possible, and she had no intention of letting him see how deeply she had been affected by his kisses, his touch, his... Oh, God, she had to get him away from here, from her!

'I think you should leave, Lyon.' God, was that huskily uncertain voice really hers? 'Now,' she added hardly.

He had recovered more quickly than her, his eyes coldly assessing as he looked down at her, a derisive twist to his lips. 'We haven't finished our negotiations—or have we...?' he added mockingly. 'I don't think my uncle would take too kindly to knowing that I could have had you here in this office this morning if I had wanted to. Do you?' He arched mocking brows.

She didn't doubt that Lyon would have taken great pleasure in telling Henry exactly that! And, if she had been the one about to marry his uncle, how destructive that would have been. But she wasn't, and, far from wanting to correct him on that assumption, she now looked forward to letting him find out the truth for himself. Arrogant, arrogant... She couldn't think of an expletive strong enough to call this man!

Her head went back proudly, her eyes flashing warningly. 'I think I'll risk Henry's reaction,' she challenged.

Lyon's eyes narrowed ominously. 'Are you that confident of his infatuation for you?' he rasped.

Silke gave him a pitying look. 'I'm that confident of the fact that he's a man, and that you're a——'

'Careful,' he warned, dangerously soft.

She shook her head derisively—as much towards herself as him; how could she have responded to such a man? He was everything she despised in a man: arrogant, self-assured to the point of condescension—in fact, too damned sure of his own power!

'I'm sure you're perfectly aware of my opinion of you,' she scorned.

His mouth twisted. 'It wasn't so apparent a few minutes ago,' he drawled challengingly.

This man used every weapon at his disposal! 'Do you know what I hope, Lyon?' There was no way she could continue to call him Mr Buchanan after the intimacy they had just shared. And they had shared it. She didn't know what excuses he was making to himself for his own part in what had happened, but she hadn't imagined his response to her. 'I hope,' she continued as he raised his brows questioningly at her, 'that I can actually be there at the moment of your humiliation. Because it's going to come,' she assured him firmly.

'I think you have that the wrong way round,' he derided.

She met his scornful gaze unflinchingly. 'We'll see,' she said softly.

'We *will* see.' He nodded abruptly, suddenly seeming to tire of the game, and straightened. 'But be warned, Silke,' he paused at the door to add. 'I rarely, if ever, lose.'

She already knew that, didn't need to be told, but this time there was no doubt he was going to lose. For her mother's sake. Her mother deserved the happiness Silke had seen in her face this morning as she sat with the man she loved. And nothing this man said or did was going to spoil that. Even if Silke had to take this man on personally to achieve that.

She shrugged. 'As I said, we'll see, Lyon.'

He scowled. 'Why are you being so damned stubborn over this, Silke?' he rasped.

'Why are you?' she returned challengingly.

'Because I can't believe you want to marry Henry. You don't even know him!' Lyon frowned darkly.

She shook her head. 'And you don't know *me*, Lyon. Not in any way that counts,' she added as he ran his gaze pointedly over the length of her body. God, even that sent a shiver of desire running down her spine. This had to stop! She didn't even like this man. And she had always believed that that was necessary in order to feel attracted towards a person. But this man had disproved that in a matter of seconds! 'I'm not getting out of Henry's life, Lyon,' she told him with certainty, sure that her mother and Henry would marry each other, and when that happened Henry would be her stepfather, and so very much in her life.

Lyon's mouth thinned ominously. 'In that case, "let battle commence",' he ground out harshly.

She gave an inclination of her head. 'By all means. Are you going to see Henry now?'

He stiffened. 'And if I am?'

'I thought I might come with you.' She picked up her handbag, ready to leave with him.

'Prepared to defend yourself?' he derided mockingly.

She shook her head confidently. 'I don't need to do that.' As he was quickly going to find out once he saw her mother at the clinic with Henry! 'Believe me, Lyon, your actions just now are more despicable than anything I'm guilty of. You're the one who attempted to make love to the woman you believe is about to marry your uncle. How do you think Henry will feel about that?' she taunted.

'He'll get over it,' he bit out confidently.

'Will he?' She raised mocking brows, preceding him from the office as he held the door open for her with a confident flourish.

This man was going to get exactly what he deserved when they got to the clinic. Arrogant, arrogant—*man*!

She refused to even allow herself to think of the fact that part of the reason she was so determined to see Lyon get his come-uppance was because she was still shaken by her own response to him...

'Frightened I might get my version in first of what happened this morning?' Lyon taunted as Silke sat beside him in the silver Mercedes on the drive to the clinic.

'Not at all,' she returned smoothly, relishing in the luxurious upholstery of the seat. 'I never drive in town, so this saves me the taxi fare!' She looked across at him with suppressed laughter in her eyes.

Lyon glanced at her briefly, frowning as he saw that laughter. 'You know,' he said slowly, 'I can't work you out.'

That must be a first for him! 'No?' She raised mocking brows. 'Maybe if you stopped looking for things that aren't there...'

'Oh, they're there, Silke.' His eyes narrowed on the road ahead. 'Your behaviour with Henry proves that.'

Her 'behaviour' with Henry was all in his imagination. Admittedly, going on what he had so far witnessed between herself and his uncle, and his uncle's subsequent claim that he was going to marry Satin, a name so similar to Silke's, even that mistake was understandable, so perhaps he felt he had reason to believe the things he did about her. But if Lyon had been a different sort of man, not so quick to judge, to arrogantly presume, then maybe someone would have corrected his wrong assumptions by now.

Although that moment wasn't far off now. Silke could hardly wait!

'You have the look of a contented cat about to partake of a bowl of cream,' Lyon suddenly barked harshly.

She hadn't realised she had given her feelings away so openly. Although that was exactly how she felt! There couldn't have been many occasions in this man's life when he had been bested, but this was definitely going to be one of them. And it couldn't have happened to a more deserving person!

Lyon watched her with narrowed eyes as she climbed out of the car to accompany him into the clinic, but Silke just met that searching scrutiny with bland indifference. She could wait for her moment of triumph.

The receptionist's comment of, 'Nice to see you again, Miss Jordan,' was received by a scowl from Lyon. Obviously he thought the receptionist was referring to Silke's having spent the previous night in Henry's room.

God, she hoped her mother hadn't left to go home and freshen up since Silke was here earlier; that would ruin everything!

She hadn't! Her mother was still sitting in the chair beside Henry's bed when Silke entered with Lyon, the older couple deep in conversation, unaware of their presence for several moments, so deeply engrossed were they with each other. It gave Silke the time to appraise her mother, to look at her as Lyon must now be doing. The similarity between the two women was unmistakable, her mother's hair as long and blonde as Silke's own, although her mother's was neatly secured at her nape. The bone-structure of their faces was the same, her mother's face animated as she talked to the man she had found again after years of being apart, her green eyes alight with happiness, both women small and slender; their relationship had to be obvious!

'My God...!' Lyon breathed slowly at her side. 'There are two of you!'

Silke looked at him with challengingly raised brows. 'Let me introduce my mother to you, Lyon,' she said smoothly. 'Tina Jordan. But I believe you may know of her as Satin,' she added tauntingly.

Lyon's stunned expression, as he looked from one woman to the other in open disbelief, was everything Silke had hoped it would be!

CHAPTER FIVE

'I STILL think we should have stayed and helped Henry explain things to his nephew.' Her mother frowned across the kitchen table at Silke, where the two women sat drinking coffee, Silke's mother having returned to her flat to shower and change before finally making an appearance at the agency.

Henry had been the one to take control of the situation at the clinic, suggesting Silke accompany her mother home while he talked to Lyon, a Lyon who predictably hadn't stayed stunned for very long, demanding an explanation. Silke's mother hadn't wanted to leave Henry alone with the irate Lyon, but Henry, possessed of a determination none of them had wanted to challenge because of his illness, had insisted that would be the best thing for everybody, shooting Silke an imploring look for her support as he did so. She had been only too happy, after her brief moment of triumph over Lyon, to suggest, as firmly as possible, that her mother leave with her. There would be plenty of time later on for her mother to come up against Lyon!

'Why don't you try explaining them to *me*?' Silke suggested gently.

Her mother looked perturbed for a moment, and then she gave a rueful grimace. 'God, yes,' she sighed. 'Everything has happened in such a rush, I'd forgotten I haven't talked to you about Hal and me.'

'Well, I know the two of you are getting married,' Silke said ruefully, never doubting that Henry intended carrying out that decision; he could be as determined as his nephew.

Her mother actually blushed at the thought of the marriage. 'At last,' she sighed self-derisively. 'God, you wouldn't believe the years I've wasted, Silke!'

She had a feeling that she would, but nevertheless she waited for her mother to tell her in her own time exactly what had happened.

Her mother shook her head. 'I was only eighteen when I met Hal, a very young eighteen at that, whereas he was already thirty-two, and a member of the Winter family. That may not mean a lot to you, darling.' She looked up at Silke as she spoke. 'But thirty-five years ago they were a family to be reckoned with: old money, a large family estate, homes all over the world, servants—you name it, they had it! And I was just an office employee of the family firm. But Hal took a liking to me, asked me out, and—well, I was attracted to him,' she said awkwardly.

'I can understand why,' Silke nodded; if Henry had looked anything like Lyon as a young man—and she had a feeling he probably had—then she could see how a young eighteen-year-old could be attracted to the powerful self-confidence he exuded, let alone the physical attributes. As she had been attracted to Lyon this morning, for different reasons! But she didn't want to think about that. 'So you went out with him,' she prompted quickly, pushing thoughts of her own reaction to Lyon to the back of her mind.

'Yes.' Her mother smiled with affection for the man she had just re-met after all those years—and discovered she still loved. Then, as other memories came back to her, she sobered. 'We went out together a few times, evenings where I was completely bowled off my feet by this fun-filled, sophisticated man. And it was a feeling that seemed to be reciprocated——'

'Why shouldn't it be?' Silke chided. 'Inverted snobbery, Mummy?' She arched blonde brows.

'You didn't know Hal's family, Silke.' Her mother shook her head, her eyes clouded. 'There was only his sister really. And her husband. An American. Charles Buchanan.' Even the way she said the name told Silke that her mother bristled with antagonism just at the thought of him.

'Lyon's father,' Silke acknowledged thoughtfully— if the father had been anything like the son, then she didn't envy her mother all those years ago!

'Yes,' her mother acknowledged with feeling, her mouth tight. 'At first, when Hal took an interest in me, they all humoured him, treated it as a huge family joke. But as time went on and they realised he was actually serious about me——! Well, I'm sure you can imagine the opposition they put up to the idea of Hal actually wanting to marry his little office girl, make her part of their family,' she said with remembered bitterness.

Once again, if Charles Buchanan had been anything like his son, Silke could imagine it all too easily. 'But Henry was a grown man of thirty-two. Surely he didn't buckle under that family pressure?' If he had, her respect for him would drop a couple of notches— and make her wonder if he was strong enough to go for what he wanted the second time around!

'No, Hal was determined to marry me, no matter what his sister and her husband felt about it.' She avoided Silke's gaze now. 'I—I was the one who did the running.' There were tears in her eyes now. 'That was the start of the running. And I've been running, in one way or another, ever since.' She shook her head in self-disgust.

'But why?' Silke looked at her searchingly. 'Henry loves you now; he must obviously have felt the same way all those years ago, so why——?'

'Charles and Marie Buchanan were killed in a car accident,' her mother said flatly. 'They left behind a six-week-old son.'

'Lyon...' Silke realised breathlessly; it was difficult to think of that autocratic man as a tiny parentless baby, completely helpless. In fact, she didn't want to think of him like that; it made him seem human!

'Lyon,' her mother confirmed with a nod. 'Hal was named as his guardian.'

That explained some of this, but by no means all of it. 'But surely Henry needed you more than ever after being left with such a small baby to care for?'

'Henry needed me; in fact our marriage had already been announced when the accident happened——'

'Then why——?'

'Charles Buchanan's family were even more powerful than Henry's.' Her mother shook her head. 'A rich Southern family, who weren't averse to using that power when it came to the Winter-Buchanan heir. And there was no way they were going to let an ex-office girl bring up that heir, so they demanded that the child be returned to them in America.'

'But Henry was his legal guardian,' Silke reasoned.

'A fact the Buchanan family disputed. They instigated a court case, claimed Henry wasn't fit to bring up a child, intending to bring up his reckless past... Oh, I knew even then that Hal had lived a far from blameless life,' she said ruefully as Silke's brows rose. 'Just as I knew he would be completely faithful to me now that we had found each other. It was that sort of love, Silke.' She smiled. 'All-consuming.' She sobered, her eyes cloudy once again. 'But they would have crucified Hal if he had married me, were completely ruthless in their determination to take the child away from him. I was the stumbling-block, Silke, and, much as I loved Hal, I—I couldn't let him give up his sister's child for me. Because the Buchanans would have won, Silke, I know it. And that knowledge would have been between us, tearing into a relationship that was already having to survive so many prejudices——'

'You would have survived as a couple, I'm sure of it,' Silke said with certainty.

'But at what price?' Her mother shook her head.

'And so you ran?' Silke frowned.

Her mother nodded. 'And so I ran,' she confirmed heavily. 'I thought Hal would get over me, that he would find someone—someone more suitable, acceptable, provide a stable home for his nephew——'

'And instead he has continued to love you. God, that's such a waste, Mummy!' Her expression was pained.

'I was eighteen, Silke. Eighteen!' Her mother looked at her pleadingly. 'I wasn't mature enough, or strong enough, to believe we could weather that legal storm. I thought it fairer to Hal not to put him through——'

'Mummy, the man has continued to love you for thirty-five years.' Silke was still stunned by the fact.

'And I've loved him too, Silke,' her mother told her quietly. 'Through the same thirty-five years, all the running, I've loved him too.'

She could see that, could see the pain etched into her mother's face at the memory of those lonely years without the man she loved. 'Perhaps—and I'm only saying perhaps—I can understand why you didn't feel able to cope with all of that at eighteen. I'm not sure any eighteen-year-old could,' she frowned. 'But later, why didn't you——?'

'I thought it would be too late,' her mother groaned. 'I told you, I thought Hal would have found someone else, had children of his own to keep Lyon company.' She shook her head. 'I never for one moment thought he would remain a bachelor.'

'Didn't you even once think of trying to find out?' Silke said incredulously, wondering if, in the same circumstances, she would have been able to do what her mother had done.

Her mother shook her head. 'I didn't dare.' Her voice broke emotionally. 'It was what I had hoped he would do, for his own sake and Lyon's, but to actually know for certain... !' she added with feeling. 'No,' she said dully. 'I never tried to find out, Silke.'

'But if you had——'

'I would never have had you,' her mother pointed out gently. 'And although I appreciate I haven't been the best mother in the world, I wouldn't have missed that experience for anything.'

Silke gave her a teasing smile. 'I'm glad you didn't! But didn't you realise,' she frowned, 'when you sent me to Buchanan's yesterday morning, that it was the same family?'

'Of course I knew it was the same family.' Her mother nodded. 'But it was a good account; I certainly didn't expect you to meet Lyon Buchanan himself! And if it hadn't been for the mistake over the bunny girl costume——'

'Could we forget about the bunny girl costume?' Silke cringed at the memory still.

'I wouldn't have met Henry again if it weren't for that costume.' Her mother shook her head.

And she wouldn't have met Lyon! 'You know, Mummy,' Silke said slowly, 'for all that I wouldn't have been born if you had married Henry all those years ago, think what a difference you could have made to Lyon as his "mother"; he's so bitter and twisted it's unbelievable!'

Her mother nodded. 'Hal would be the first to admit he didn't do a very good job of bringing Lyon up on his own. A question of a cynic bringing up a cynic! Hal was very upset after I left.' She grimaced. 'Didn't relish the idea of caring for a small baby, left it to hired staff most of the time. And while Lyon was growing up there were apparently always too many women interested in that vast Winter-Buchanan fortune that he inherited the majority of when he reached twenty-one.'

Silke could easily believe that, and was sure that Lyon had little idea what the 'real world' and 'real people' were like, that his cynicism owed more to the women he had met in his life than to the way Henry had brought him up. He had lived in too rarefied an atmosphere to appreciate that there were women in the world who wouldn't want him for his money and the prestige of being his wife. But she didn't want to

be one of those women, didn't want to want him—
in any way!

'Hal and Satin?' she prompted teasingly, anxious
to put all thoughts of Lyon from her mind now.

Her mother blushed becomingly. 'Hal is obvious,
I think. Satin because—well, Hal always said I had
skin like satin.' Her blush deepened. 'The years
haven't been that kind to me.' She grimaced. 'So he's
going to find I'm not quite as——'

'Mummy, the man loves you,' Silke cut in protestingly. 'He isn't going to worry about things like that.
And neither should you.'

But Silke had to admit that *she* was worried; Lyon
was going to be in her life for a long time to come.
And after her reaction to him this morning, she wasn't
sure how she was going to deal with that.

It was like waiting for the sword of Damocles to drop.
Three days. Three days since Henry Winter had told
Lyon that he was going to marry her mother. Three
days in which there had been complete silence from
the man himself.

And Silke didn't like it. Not one little bit. Her
mother seemed to think she was worrying unnecessarily, that Henry's talk with the younger man had obviously proved fruitful, but Silke's own encounters
with the man led her to believe otherwise. She didn't
believe for a moment that Lyon was going to accept
this situation with the calm indifference he appeared
to be.

She was right!

'For someone who "doesn't even work at the
agency" you seem to spend an awful lot of time here,'
drawled a mockingly derisive voice.

Silke looked up sharply from her seat behind her mother's desk where she had been working, looking across the room at Lyon. As usual he had walked in unannounced. 'Don't you ever knock, Lyon?' she scorned as she closed the file she had been working on, to give him her full attention; she would be a fool to do anything else where this man was concerned!

He closed the door softly behind him, shutting out the hovering Jackie; the other woman looked apologetic at the fact that she had been unable to stop this man doing exactly as he liked. Again. At least, she *had* looked apologetic, until the door was firmly closed in her face!

'I came to see your mother,' Lyon told Silke dismissively, brows raised at the fact that she obviously wasn't here.

But Silke was. 'And doesn't she deserve your respect either?' she challenged, unnerved at having him walk in here, even though she had been half expecting to hear from him.

His mouth tightened as he crossed the room. 'Where is she? No—let me guess; playing the loving fiancée at the clinic with Henry?' he scorned.

Silke gave him a pitying look. 'She isn't "playing" anything, Lyon. My mother happens to love your uncle. And, more importantly,' she added as she could see he was about to make a scathing reply, 'your uncle loves her.'

Lyon sat down in the chair opposite her, placing a large brown envelope on the desk in front of him. 'Henry is an old man; he doesn't even——'

'Don't be so damned patronising!' Silke snapped angrily, getting to her feet, looking very slim in fitted black trousers and a soft green jumper. 'My God, you make him sound ten degrees off being senile!' she accused heatedly, eyes blazing indignantly, having become very fond, during the last three days, of the man who was about to become her stepfather. She certainly had no intention of standing by and listening to Lyon denigrate him.

'At the moment that's exactly how he's behaving!' Lyon rasped back, looking at her coldly between narrowed lids. 'My God, he calmly announces to me that he's about to marry a woman he hasn't even seen for thirty-five years, and I'm supposed to accept that he's completely in control of his faculties!' He shook his head disbelievingly.

Silke glared at him. 'You aren't supposed to accept anything, Lyon,' she told him disgustedly. 'They're two grown adults, with——'

'Who have suddenly "found each other" again after all these years?' Lyon derided contemptuously. 'Spare me that, Silke,' he scorned. 'Henry may never have married, but he's hardly lived a celibate life the last thirty-five years——'

'No one is claiming that he has,' she defended, her whole body taut with indignation, her hands clenched at her sides. Just who did this man think he was, talking about her mother and Henry in this way?

'—and your mother's life has hardly been blameless either,' Lyon continued firmly. Pointedly.

She became suddenly still, her expression wary now as she looked at him. 'I beg your pardon?' she prompted softly.

His mouth twisted. 'Your mother's life, over the last thirty-five years, makes interesting reading,' he told her challengingly, dark brows raised.

Silke frowned down at him—before glancing across the desk at the brown envelope he had put down so pointedly on his arrival. He suddenly took on the appearance of a cobra about to strike!

She couldn't believe it. This man, this—this... Words failed her as to describing exactly what he was. How dared he have her mother's past investigated? Because Silke knew, with sickening clarity, that was exactly what Lyon had done, that *this* was the reason for his silence of the last three days.

'You're despicable!' she finally told him disgustedly. 'Absolutely beneath contempt!'

She could imagine all too clearly how that report on her mother would read, knew how her mother's life would sound written down in black and white, the flitting from job to job, country to country, the finally settling down for two years with Silke's father, seeming barely to give birth to Silke before she was off again, this time dragging her child around with her. There had been relationships with men before Silke was born, other relationships in the years that followed her birth. Once she was old enough to understand, her mother had been completely honest with her about those, and, loving her as she did, Silke had accepted her mother's life.

But baldly written down on paper, without her mother's emotions to back it up, it would all look very irresponsible, probably promiscuous too. Which, looking at Lyon's contemptuous expression, was exactly what it looked like to him. Damn the man!

'Henry has a right to know about the woman he says he wants to marry,' Lyon told her tightly in answer to her accusation.

Silke glared at him, angry on her mother's behalf. 'Anything your uncle wants to know about my mother, she will tell him.'

'Will she?'

Silke bristled even more at Lyon's sceptical tone. 'Yes!' In fact, she was sure her mother and Henry had done little else but talk the last three days, that and arrange a special licence so that they could be married as soon as the other arrangements could be made. Which this man probably knew nothing about. And which Silke, after what he had just said about her mother, had no intention of telling him, either! 'Tell me, Lyon, what's happened in your life to make you so damned cynical?' she challenged.

God, she was more than a little cynical herself after James had let her down so badly, but that didn't stop her feeling happy for her mother and Henry—it just meant she had no intention of ever falling in love again herself!

Lyon stiffened at the familiarity of the question. 'We weren't discussing me——'

'Oh, but I think we were.' Silke shook her head, her hair a silver-blonde frame to gamin features. 'It seems to me that it's your own experiences with relationships that is making you judge the past situation between Henry and my mother; that you——'

'Don't try any of your amateur psychology on me, Silke,' Lyon scorned harshly. 'The Winter-Buchanan money has always been the draw——'

'My mother gave all that up once,' she pointed out softly, looking at him searchingly; was it possible this man had been through a similar experience to her own, that he had also been let down in love? But she didn't want to have anything in common with Lyon!

Certainly didn't want to find they had an affinity because of past hurts. Considering the physical reaction there seemed to be between them—no matter how much they both wished it weren't there!—that could be dangerous, very dangerous...

Lyon shrugged now. 'She was young at the time, didn't realise quite what she was giving up. Besides, when it came down to it, she obviously didn't want the responsibility of someone else's brat!' His mouth twisted with distaste. 'I doubt taking on someone else's baby with the wedding-ring was the lifestyle she had in mind at all!'

Silke frowned. 'Is that really what you think happened?'

'Don't be so bloody naïve, Silke; of course that's what happened!' he scorned.

She shook her head again. 'That explanation doesn't make sense either, Lyon; with all that Winter-Buchanan money at her disposal my mother wouldn't have had to have anything to do with you herself if she didn't want to. She could have paid people to do that!'

'Henry wouldn't have allowed that——'

'Henry did it!' she reasoned forcefully, clearly remembering the conversation between the two men on that first day. And Lyon might not like her 'amateur psychology', but it was becoming more and more obvious, despite Henry's efforts—and that damned Winter-Buchanan money!—that Lyon had always had a very lonely life.

'Because he had no choice,' Lyon bit out harshly now, eyes glittering dangerously. 'He was a man on his own, with a business to run——'

'If you know that, why do you give him such a hard time over your childhood?' she prompted softly. Her own childhood hadn't exactly been 'normal' either, and her experience with James hadn't been fun, but she was sure she didn't have the same cynical approach to life Lyon did. Did she...?

He stood up forcefully, glaring down at her, a nerve pulsing in one tightly clenched cheek. 'Silke, I don't discuss my personal affairs with anyone like this,' he finally ground out dismissively.

Maybe that was his problem. When James had walked out on her she hadn't hidden herself away and licked her wounds, had talked and talked and talked, mainly to her mother, until she had talked a lot of the pain and disillusionment away. None of the talking had really changed the situation; James had still betrayed her in the worst possible way, the wedding-dress hanging in her bedroom seeming to mock her until she had got rid of it, but at least she hadn't kept all the bitterness inside her, destroying her. As it was, this man...

'Maybe you should try it some time, Lyon,' she said lightly.

Dark brows rose over scornful eyes. 'With you?'

She looked shocked, moving away from him to sit back in her chair behind the desk, as far away from Lyon as she possibly could be. No, not with her! This man disturbed her enough already, had broken down certain of her defences she would rather have remained intact. She didn't want to know the man behind the hard façade, felt far safer telling herself that there wasn't one, that this hard, cynical man was all there was.

'Certainly not,' she snapped defensively. 'As you so rightly guessed, my mother is at the clinic with Henry. Go and do your worst with the information you have on her. I can guarantee it won't make any difference to either of them,' she added confidently.

Lyon shook his head. 'There are no guarantees in this world, Silke,' he rasped abruptly.

She had thought her relationship with James the sort that would last a lifetime—and look how badly that had turned out! If James hadn't run off in the way that he had, they would have been married almost a year by now, a year she had believed would be filled with the happiness of setting up home together, of discovering all those things about each other that it wasn't possible to know until you actually lived with someone. And instead——

'But you look as if you already know that,' Lyon said quietly, having moved to stand beside her now.

Silke gave him a startled look, wondering just how much she had revealed in those few disturbed moments. Too much, if Lyon's searching gaze was anything to go by! The last thing she wanted—next to not getting to know the man behind the façade!—was for *him* to get to know *her*!

'I'm twenty-five, Lyon,' she dismissed with deliberate flippancy. 'You don't get to that age without realising that the saying "life can be a bitch" is founded on a certain amount of truth!'

His mouth twisted. 'I believe the correct saying is "life's a bitch—and then you die"!'

'Oh, let's be correct.' She gave a mocking inclination of her head.

He gave a grim smile. 'I think the most interesting part of that statement is that life is classed as being female.'

'Careful, Lyon,' Silke drawled, her equilibrium regained after her brief lapse. 'Or you could be mistaken for a misogynist!' She looked at him challengingly.

Dark brows rose. 'I don't dislike women, Silke,' he told her softly.

'No?' she taunted sceptically.

'No.' His mouth firmed. 'I don't know what Henry has told you about me—and I don't particularly want to know, either—but I think I should warn you he gets annoyed because I won't confide my private life to him, and because I won't he chooses to believe I don't have one. He's never accepted the fact that I've grown up!'

Silke quirked blonde brows. 'Does any parent?' She shrugged. 'You'll probably be the same yourself when you have children of your own.' Good God, how had they progressed from outright antagonism to discussing this man's prospective children!

He obviously thought the same thing, giving a disgusted snort. 'I doubt it,' he drawled non-committally. 'In the meantime, I have no intention of the two of *us* ever being related!'

Discussion over, Silke thought as she stiffened at his intended insult; after all, she was the daughter of the woman he believed to be a gold-digger, and he had no intention of showing her even politeness, let alone talking to her! 'Talk to Henry and my mother about that, not me!' she snapped.

Lyon looked grim now. 'I intend to! It's ridiculous for them to imagine they still love each other after all these years; they don't even know each other, only a memory!'

And this man intended to make sure they realised that! Silke didn't agree with him—but then, when had she?—and she believed, no matter what happened, that her mother and Henry were adults, and as such should be left to make their own choices—or mistakes, if that was what they turned out to be.

She shook her head. 'I don't think that's any of our business——'

'I'm sure you don't,' Lyon rasped scornfully, looking about him disparagingly. 'Your mother certainly wouldn't have to concern herself with this place if she were Henry's wife.'

Silke gave him a pitying look. 'And no doubt you're the sort of man who would insist on your future wife's signing a prenuptial agreement before you would condescend to go through with the wedding!'

'Not at all,' he drawled, dark brows raised mockingly as Silke looked up at him. 'For the simple reason that I never intend falling into the marriage trap!'

Was that really what it was, what it had become? She had looked forward to her marriage to James, had anticipated their happiness together. No, despite what had happened to her engagement to James, she couldn't agree with Lyon's sentiments on marriage. Although at the same time she couldn't see herself ever contemplating it again either. But for her mother and Henry it was a different matter...

'Obviously Henry and my mother don't feel the same way about it that you do,' she dismissed. 'And I really don't think you have the right to interfere.'

Lyon's eyes were glacial. 'I have the right to protect Henry from his own folly!' he bit out harshly.

Silke raised blonde brows at his arrogance. 'Do you?'

'Yes!' he rasped forcefully. 'So be prepared to pick up the pieces!' He marched over to the door, a man totally in command of a situation.

'Er—Lyon...?' Silke called out to him softly as he reached the door.

He turned back to her, his brows challengingly raised.

'You forgot this.' Her mouth twisted disgustedly as she held up the brown envelope he had placed so confidently on her desk a short time ago. Containing damaging evidence against her mother, she was sure. She was also sure her mother and Henry had become strong enough together the last few days to withstand anything Lyon had to throw at them.

But at the same time she knew she had to warn them of what Lyon was trying to do, waiting until Lyon had grabbed up the brown envelope from her to stride forcefully from the room before placing a call through to the clinic.

To her surprise she was told that Mr Winter had been discharged that morning. Silke very much doubted Lyon was aware of that. Or that his temper, or his determination, would be improved by not knowing!

Her mother wasn't answering the telephone at her apartment either, which meant she was probably at Henry's home with him. And Silke had no idea where that was. Oh, well, she had tried to let them know of Lyon's intention of causing trouble. And she couldn't really believe, after seeing the older couple together the last few days, that Henry and her mother would be affected by anything Lyon had to say on the subject of her mother's past. Maybe someone would even get around to telling Lyon that he, for different reasons from the ones he was assuming, was the reason her mother had fled from the situation all those years ago.

Why hadn't she told Lyon the truth this morning? He had certainly given her the perfect opening for it. And yet she hadn't taken it. Why hadn't she?

The truth was, she didn't want to probe her own motives too deeply! He seemed to have no hesitation in trampling over other people's feelings, so why——?

The less she thought about Lyon, the better. Determinedly opening the next file on her desk, intent on forgetting about him, she concentrated on her work. Unfortunately, the next account she looked at was the one for Buchanan's for the hire of the bunny girl. The wrong bunny girl. God, Silke still cringed when she thought of that day and that damned outfit she had been wearing. She doubted Buchanan's would forget it in a hurry either!

This time she didn't even look surprised when Lyon burst into the office a short time later, and there was certainly no point in being annoyed about it; it seemed to be becoming a habit of his!

As usual he didn't bother to knock, just walked in. As if he owned the place. As if she didn't have any work to do.

She looked up at him with weary resignation. 'Yes, Lyon?'

'Did you know about it all the time?' he demanded without preliminaries, towering over her as he stood by the desk.

Silke instantly felt irritated by this man's constant superiority over her. Not that it would make an awful lot of difference if she were to stand up, she realised ruefully; he would still dwarf her! He——

'Well?' he demanded harshly at her lack of response. 'Did you know?'

Obviously he had been to the clinic and knew of his uncle's discharge. And he was furious about it. Good God, could no one make a move without this man's permission?

'I telephoned the clinic after you left earlier.' She nodded. 'Don't look so worried, Lyon,' she chided as he still scowled darkly. 'I'm sure they wouldn't have discharged Henry if he weren't well enough to——'

'Peter didn't discharge him,' Lyon cut in harshly, eyes blazing. 'Henry discharged himself!'

Silke frowned at this news. Although even that wasn't too serious, surely; Henry had seemed fine when she saw him the previous evening, and Peter Carruthers had originally said the older man only needed a few days' bed-rest. It didn't seem too disastrous to her that Henry had tired of the clinic and decided to take matters into his own hands. Although she could see that it bothered Lyon enormously!

'Where are they, Silke?' he rasped, his eyes taking on a silver sheen. 'And don't say you don't know, because I can't believe your mother hasn't invited you to the wedding,' he added accusingly.

Wedding? But that wasn't until next week, when—when they could be sure Henry was out of hospital...

Silke stared up at Lyon, a terrible truth starting to dawn on her; her mother and Henry had decided to avoid any further confrontation with Lyon and had gone off somewhere quietly and got married. That was the reason Henry had discharged himself without anyone knowing!

CHAPTER SIX

'WELL?' Lyon demanded as she continued staring at him.

Well, indeed. What could she say? She knew exactly what her mother and Henry had done—and she couldn't blame them in the least. Not in the circumstances. The last thing Henry needed at the moment was tension and strain, and dealing with Lyon over this situation was sure to cause that. Much better simply to present him with a *fait accompli*. Lyon was aware of that too—and he was obviously absolutely furious at the idea of being duped by the older couple.

'Well,' Silke repeated slowly, leaning back in her chair, playing for time really. What could she say? She didn't know any of the details of her mother and Henry's disappearance, only appreciated the reason for it. But at the same time she knew Lyon wasn't going to believe her ignorance about the older couple's plans.

'Where are they, Silke?' Lyon ground out harshly at her continued silence.

She looked at him consideringly, at his set features, the cold fury in his eyes—and she was grateful she knew none of the details of the runaways' wedding. Because she knew that, if she had, Lyon wouldn't have relented until he had extracted those details from her. Which she was sure her mother and Henry were aware of too.

She drew in a deep breath. 'I know you aren't going to believe this——'

'If you're about to tell me you don't know where Henry and your mother are, then no, I'm not,' Lyon grated, eyes glittering.

Silke grimaced at his determined expression. 'I don't know where Henry and my mother are,' she repeated evenly, her own gaze unflinching.

He let out a controlled snort of disbelief. 'Silke, you——' He broke off as the telephone on the desk began to ring. 'Instruct your secretary to hold all calls,' he bit out harshly, glaring balefully at the offending telephone.

Silke arched blonde brows at him at the same time as she reached out for the receiver. 'I have a business to run, Lyon, and——'

'It's your mother's business,' he snapped. 'And after today it doesn't look as if she's going to need it any more!'

Silke picked up the receiver, her gaze never leaving Lyon's determinedly set face as he moved to sit in the chair facing her desk. Not that he looked in the least relaxed once he had sat down, his body filled with a powerful tension as he sat so quietly watching her. Unnerving!

What was even more unnerving was the voice on the other end of the telephone line! No wonder Jackie hadn't hesitated in putting the call through!

'Silke! Darling, I——'

'Hello, Mrs—Adams.' There was only the slightest hesitation before the surname—thank God. The last thing she wanted was for Lyon to realise it was her mother on the telephone! As it was, her own palms were sweating as she held the receiver, and she was sure she must have gone slightly pale. 'No, my mother isn't here at the moment,' she said pointedly; Lyon was the one who was here! 'I believe she's getting married today,' she added even more pointedly, frowning warily as Lyon instantly looked furious.

'Who's there with you, Silke?'

Thank goodness her mother had picked up on the near panic of her words, even if she had managed to keep her tone lightly friendly! 'Your guess is as good as mine,' she replied dismissively. Guess, Mummy, guess! Who else but Lyon Buchanan would make her behave in this way?

'Lyon,' her mother realised heavily. 'He's been to the clinic?'

'Yes,' Silke replied economically.

'Oh, God, Silke,' her mother sighed. 'I'm so sorry. Is he very angry?'

'Very,' she confirmed lightly, a brief glance at Lyon's face telling her his mood wasn't being improved by the interruption of this telephone call. And that was without even realising who the caller actually was!

'We thought this way was for the best, Silke,' her mother explained apologetically.

'I'm sure you're right,' she quickly assured her; the longer this call continued, the more short-tempered Lyon was likely to become—and he was difficult enough to deal with already. 'I'll tell my mother you called,' she briskly decided to conclude the conversation as she saw Lyon move in his chair impatiently. 'Perhaps you could call back?'

'Tonight, Silke,' her mother instantly agreed. 'At my apartment?'

'That would be best,' Silke agreed in a relieved tone.

'Are you all right, Silke?' her mother said worriedly. 'God knows I realise how obnoxious Lyon can be——'

'I'm just running things for my mother while she's away,' she cut in quickly, sure from the increasing displeasure on Lyon's face that he was actually going to wrench the receiver out of her hand in a minute and tell 'Mrs Adams' to go to hell. And once he had spoken to her mother that would ruin everything! 'We'll look forward to hearing from you.' She rang off quickly before her mother could say anything else, putting down the receiver as if it were red-hot.

At which Lyon instantly reached out and pressed the internal button. 'No more calls,' he barked to Jackie when she answered the call, looking across challengingly at Silke as she watched him with raised brows.

She glared at him. 'Make yourself at home, why don't you?' she said sarcastically.

'Our conversation is more important than your mother's clients,' he snapped icily.

'In your opinion,' Silke drawled, sitting back in her chair. At least she had heard from her mother, no longer had to wonder about that particular situation. And she would talk to her again later in the day. Lyon didn't have that reassurance.

His eyes flashed. 'Aren't you in the least concerned that your mother has just disappeared with my uncle? Stupid question,' he dismissed disgustedly, his mouth twisted contemptuously. 'Once the two of them are married——'

'Don't say it, Lyon,' she warned sharply, no longer quite as relaxed, green eyes flashing warningly.

His mouth twisted scathingly. 'The benefits of becoming Henry's stepdaughter can't have escaped you!'

She looked across at him with narrowed eyes. 'At the moment the only thing I can think of in connection with that marriage is that it somehow makes the two of us related—and I can't see that as any sort of benefit at all!' In fact, quite the opposite. Especially with the physical effect this man, unwillingly, had on her! Coming into contact with him on a regular basis was—well, it was unthinkable.

'No?' Lyon arched dark brows. 'Is that why Henry has been extolling the genius of your jewellery designs?'

Silke looked at him sharply, frowning deeply. 'As far as I'm aware, Henry hasn't seen any of my designs...' What on earth was Lyon talking about?

'Exactly,' Lyon drawled.

Her frown deepened. 'What do you mean?'

He shook his head derisively. 'Henry wouldn't need to have seen your designs to have decided you're a genius—as far as he's concerned at the moment, anyone connected with his wonderful Satin can do no wrong!' And it was obvious he didn't share his uncle's opinion—in fact, the opposite!

Silke's mind was racing; why on earth had Henry been praising her jewellery designs—designs she was positive he hadn't even seen! Surely he couldn't—he wouldn't—— She looked up at Lyon with wide, startled eyes as she realised that Henry would!

Lyon raised mocking brows, grey eyes scathing. 'Don't tell me you aren't aware of the fact that Henry believes Buchanan's should branch out with its own jewellery designs?' he scorned.

Her stomach lurched, her face paling; Henry had! Oh, God! Of course she had had no idea. She wouldn't have let Henry... Let him? It wasn't a question of letting Henry do anything, he was turning out to be as arrogantly determined to have his own way as his nephew was, albeit in a more charmingly persuasive way. She was sure it hadn't been her mother's idea to go off and get married in the way they were; her mother had been quite prepared to fight Lyon herself on his own terms. Henry's determinedly persuasive hand had to have been behind that move too, Silke was sure of it. Henry's only saving grace at the moment, as far as Silke was concerned, was that she didn't doubt his love for her mother, or that he would do everything in his power to ensure her happiness. Including setting her daughter up in business ... !

Lyon's gaze raked over her appraisingly, finally settling on the now pale beauty of her face. 'I don't recall ever seeing you wear jewellery yourself...?' he finally said pointedly.

Her designs were more of the chunky costume jewellery kind, not the sort of thing she could wear in the day with jeans and T-shirts, her usual daytime wear. Besides, the state of her personal finances, she couldn't even afford to produce samples of her designs in the gold and silver needed. But Buchanan's could... No! She had no intention of encouraging Henry in this mad scheme. Of opposing Lyon...

'I——' She broke off her protest as the telephone on her desk began to ring for the second time during this meeting.

Lyon scowled his displeasure at the interruption. 'I thought I told your secretary no more calls?' And he wasn't used to having his instructions disobeyed, his tone clearly implied.

And normally Jackie wouldn't have dreamt of disobeying them either, which told Silke there had to be a good reason for her having done so now. Her mother calling again...? Didn't she know Lyon well enough to realise Silke wouldn't have managed to get rid of him yet?

She almost panicked completely as Lyon, tiring of waiting for her to answer the call, reached out for the receiver, and she snatched it up herself first, avoiding his gaze as she turned away. 'Yes, Jackie?' she responded huskily.

'Silke,' Jackie sounded breathless herself. 'James is on the line.'

James? James...! Her James? No, not her James, not if it was the same James who had walked out of her life a year ago and married someone else on the eve of their own wedding. It couldn't be that James!

'James Cameron, Silke,' Jackie instantly confirmed that indeed it could be! 'And he says it's urgent that he talk to you,' she added by way of explanation for this interruption when she had been given clear instructions, albeit by Lyon Buchanan, not to put any more calls through.

Urgent? After almost a year of complete silence James had found something urgent to talk to her about? He had to be joking! Besides, whatever his problem was, she certainly had no intention of taking his call now, not with Lyon Buchanan sitting across the desk from her so watchfully.

'Get his telephone number and tell him I'll call him back, Jackie,' she instructed—God, was that shaky voice really hers?

But maybe she could be excused that; this was certainly turning out to be a traumatic day, with first Lyon on the warpath, and now James on the telephone—for goodness' knew what reason. Perhaps he wanted them to get together to celebrate what should have been the first anniversary of their wedding-day? God, she was becoming hysterical now, she realised; but how else could she feel in the circumstances? Today was turning into a nightmare!

'I would have reprimanded her for her inefficiency,' Lyon rasped once Silke had put down the receiver.

'Well, that's where we differ,' Silke replied without her usual fight where this man was concerned—she was still shaken by James's call. A year, a whole year of silence; why was he calling her now? He had been away on his honeymoon with someone else when she had cancelled their wedding, their honeymoon, sent back the unwanted wedding gifts; he hadn't wanted to know, hadn't cared about her pain, her humiliation, her——

'Him?' Lyon prompted, grey eyes narrowed questioningly on the paleness of her face when Silke looked up at him almost dazedly.

She frowned, swallowing hard. What had the two of them been talking about before her telephone call from James? She had no intention of telling Lyon who 'him' was! She could all too easily imagine his derision if she told him about James, her ex-fiancé who had married someone else on the eve of their wedding!

She forced her expression to become coolly dismissive. 'I believe we were discussing Henry's interest in my jewellery designs,' she prompted pointedly.

'No,' Lyon said slowly. 'We were discussing the fact that you never wear jewellery yourself.' His narrowed gaze moved to the bareness of her hands as they rested on the desktop.

Was it her imagination, or did that all-seeing gaze rest more intently on the bareness of her left hand, where until a year ago an emerald and diamond engagement ring had nestled on the third finger? A ring that had been returned to James along with everything else once the wedding had been cancelled; she hadn't wanted anything left in her flat to remind her of James and their engagement. She could still remember the feeling of desolation as she parcelled up the box that had contained all her memories of the years she had spent with James; it had seemed so little to show for three years of her life. And now, with one simple telephone call, the memories were back ... At a time when she could least deal with it; Lyon Buchanan was seated opposite her, obviously on the warpath!

And even though she was sure there could be no evidence that she had once worn an engagement ring on her left hand, the indentation that had once been there having long gone, she found herself putting that hand beneath the desk, where Lyon could no longer see it.

'You're quite wrong,' she told Lyon coolly now. 'I often wear jewellery; you've just never met me in the right setting to see me wearing it.' Even as she said it, Silke winced, remembering all too vividly—as she was sure Lyon did!—the circumstances in which they had first met; she had been wearing very little on that occasion, and certainly no jewellery.

Lyon looked at her thoughtfully, grey eyes narrowed. 'Then perhaps I should rectify that,' he finally said slowly.

Silke gave him a startled look. 'What do you mean?'

He shrugged those broad shoulders. 'It seems I can do little to stop this wedding between my uncle and your mother—so perhaps the two of us should have dinner together this evening to celebrate their marriage.'

Silke looked at him suspiciously; why had he suddenly changed from opposing the marriage to suggesting they go out and celebrate it? He was suddenly being altogether too pleasant—and Silke distrusted this mood even more than she did his outright objectionable one.

She shook her head. 'I don't think so——'

'Frightened, Silke?' he taunted softly.

She frowned at the suggestion. 'Of what?'

'Me,' he derided, brows raised mockingly.

And suddenly she was—of the fact that he realised how physically vulnerable she was towards him. And why shouldn't he? She had hardly beaten him off with a stick on the occasions he had taken her into his arms and kissed her!

Both her hands were beneath the desktop now—to hide the fact that they were shaking. First James, and now this man; it was too much in one day!

She forced herself to meet his gaze unflinchingly. 'I'm not frightened of you, Lyon.' Her voice was steady too, determinedly so.

He gave an acknowledging nod of his head, his mouth quirked mockingly. 'In that case——' he stood up in one fluid movement '—I take it you have no objection to joining me for dinner this evening? I'll pick you up——'

'Now just a minute,' Silke cut in hastily. 'I'm not frightened of you, Lyon—why on earth should I be?' she added with impatient dismissal. 'But neither do I want to have dinner with you, tonight or at any other time,' she said exasperatedly.

He towered over her, looking down at her, those dark brows still mockingly raised. 'Careful, Silke,' he taunted. 'You're starting to sound like a woman who protests too much! Now I suggest——'

'That must be a novelty for you!' she snapped impatiently.

'—that I call for you at your flat at seven-thirty,' he continued as if she hadn't made the interruption. 'That way we'll have time for a drink before dinner. Unless you intend being at your mother's apartment? You seem to spend as much time there as you do at your own home,' he added drily.

'How do you——?' Silke broke off abruptly, glaring at him. 'Of course, your report on my mother. Or was it just on my mother?' she suddenly realised warily. My God, he wouldn't have had her investigated too, would he? What a stupid question; of course he would—this man was arrogant enough to do anything he wanted to do! Maybe she hadn't been so wrong about his lingering gaze on her left hand earlier, after all...

Lyon calmly met her gaze. 'Seven-thirty, Silke,' he repeated smoothly. 'At your own or your mother's apartment?'

'I told you,' she snapped, completely flustered by her racing thoughts as to what his report had told him about her. 'Neither!' She glared up at him.

He bent forward, his face only inches from hers now as he leant over the desk. 'I may—regrettably—have lost one battle today, Silke.' His breath softly stirred her wispy blonde fringe. 'I have no intention of losing this one too,' he added grimly.

As she doubted he actually intended losing the war; she had no doubts whatsoever that Henry's and her mother's battle with him was far from over. Lyon was just retreating slightly in order to rally his troops. And Silke didn't want to be caught in the firing line!

'I'm busy tonight, Lyon,' she told him firmly—and every other night as far as this man was concerned. He was far too dangerous for her peace of mind!

'Cancel it,' he instructed arrogantly.

She gasped. 'I——'

'I'll be at your mother's apartment at seven-thirty, Silke.' He walked over to the door. 'We can discuss your jewellery designs over dinner.'

As carrots went it was far from subtle; but then Lyon Buchanan had never been subtle where she was concerned. She doubted he was ever subtle with anyone; he didn't need to be, was far too powerful ever to need to be. But Silke wasn't interested in anything he had to say about her jewellery designs—if indeed that was what he actually wanted to talk about, which she doubted; no doubt he still believed she knew where his uncle and her mother were!—because she could never work for this man. Never!

And she didn't want him coming to her mother's apartment at seven-thirty, either; what if her mother hadn't rung by then and happened to ring once Lyon had arrived to pick her up? God, no, she didn't want that!

'My designs are all at my flat——'

'Then I'll call for you there,' he nodded, opening the door. 'Seven-thirty,' he repeated as if to a backward child, before striding arrogantly from the office.

Silke was left sitting behind her mother's desk opening and closing her mouth like a floundering fish. She had been about to tell him that her designs were all at her flat but that she had no intention of having dinner with him anyway. But he hadn't let her finish. Had railroaded over her objections. As he seemed to do with everyone, she realised, as she saw Jackie sitting behind her desk with a similarly dazed expression on her face as she watched Lyon's departure.

Jackie turned her head slowly, and the two women looked at each other for several long seconds, both looking totally bewildered.

Finally Jackie shook her head. 'I don't know what it is about that man, but he—well, he——'

'It's all right, Jackie,' Silke sympathised, running an exasperated hand through the length of her hair. 'He has the same effect on everyone.' And she appeared to be stuck with going out to dinner with the man; how was she going to get through the evening?

'Here's that telephone number you asked for, Silke.' Jackie stood in front of her desk, holding out a piece of paper towards her.

Silke blinked up at her, completely puzzled for a few seconds—and then she remembered. James! How could she have forgotten that he had telephoned? Lyon Buchanan, that was how! He was enough to drive every other thought from anyone's mind—even that of an ex-fiancé who had contacted her after a year of silence—and almost a year of his being married to someone else!

My God, James had a nerve after all this time. What on earth could they have to say to each other now? The truth was, she had nothing to say to him. She had wanted to say it all a year ago and hadn't been given the chance; now it was all totally irrelevant, even her pain and anger towards him having faded to a mild contempt for the way he had behaved.

She stared down at the piece of paper with his telephone number on long after Jackie had returned to her own outer office, vaguely registering the fact that James still worked for the same firm of accountants. Some things didn't change, she acknowledged with wry self-derision. But she had, and James contacting her now was nothing more than an irritation. An irritation she could well have done without with Lyon Buchanan present!

Finally she opened her handbag and put the piece of paper with the telephone number inside her purse. Whatever James wanted to talk to her about, it could wait; it had already waited a year, so it couldn't be that urgent.

The urgent thing on her mind at the moment was the thought of dinner with Lyon Buchanan. What was he up to? Because she didn't for one minute believe the two of them were about to celebrate his uncle's and her mother's marriage. Or that he was seriously interested in her jewellery designs . . .

There was absolutely nothing Silke could do about her mother's expected telephone call at her apartment. The only complication Silke could see was that once her mother received no reply at her own apartment she would then try Silke's flat. As Silke luxuriated in a much-needed relaxing bath once she got in from the office, she could only hope her mother called before Lyon arrived. Although the way her luck was going at the moment, she very much doubted that would be the case!

She had firmly put the subject of James to the back of her mind—at least for the evening. He had waited this long; he could certainly wait another day!

The first thing Silke had done when she got in from work had been to look through her wardrobe for something to wear to go out with Lyon, something smart and elegant, but nothing that gave him the impression she had wanted to look beautiful for him; he would be sure to comment on something so obvious. But the truth of the matter was she did want him to find her attractive; the few occasions they had met he had hardly seen her in a good light, and she needed all the ammunition she had to withstand an evening spent in that particular man's company.

The dress she had finally settled on was just a plain black, with a high neckline, and long sleeves. But the material was of a type that moulded to her body rather than clung, and the short length, just above her knee, allowed for a long expanse of her shapely legs. Yes, it was just the right sort of dress to wear to go out with Lyon Buchanan, provocative without being suggestive.

And because of the plainness of the dress she would be able to complement it with some of the jewellery he had commented he had never seen her wear, the dress being perfect for the chunky style of her designs.

Lyon Buchanan would see a completely different Silke Jordan tonight, one who was as sophisticated and self-assured as the women he usually associated with! It was ridiculous that she had to go to these lengths at all, she knew, but she had been forced into going out for the dinner in the first place, and she needed every weapon available to her to get through it. God, there she went with the warlike vocabulary again. But that was exactly what it had felt like since she first met Lyon!

But she forgot all about war and battles and weapons when the doorbell rang shrilly at a quarter past seven; Lyon was early! She wasn't even ready, had already laddered one pair of sheer tights and had to search frantically for another pair. Of which she had only smoothed up one leg!

The doorbell rang again—more insistently this time? Damn him, he was fifteen minutes early; as well as not being dressed, she hadn't yet applied her make-up or even attempted to brush her hair. Had he done this on purpose, as a deliberate attempt to disconcert her before the evening even began? She wouldn't put it past him!

She was flushed and cross by the time she reached the door after its third ring, having frantically pulled the tights off because she didn't have time to smooth them on, only succeeding in laddering that pair too as one of her nails broke in her rush. Lyon had succeeded in more than disconcerting her; she was furious with him for trying to put her at a disadvantage!

'Stop ringing the damned——' All of Silke's anger disappeared into mind-blowing disbelief as she opened the door to find, not Lyon standing on the doorstep, but James! What on earth——?

'Silke,' he said quietly, looking down at her intently.

Damn it, why did he have to be another tall man, able to look down at her with his male superiority? It was totally illogical to Silke at that moment to accept that she would be hard pushed to find any man shorter than her own five feet; also that James's height of over six feet had been one of the things that had attracted her to him in the first place. He had no right being here at all now, height or no height!

She glared up at him, at the man she had once loved, intended to marry—and knew that whatever she had once felt for him was completely dead. He was just a tall, attractive man, his blond hair slightly longer than she remembered, a few more lines beside the dark blue eyes; but just a tall, attractive man, after all. Silke certainly felt no residual love for him.

'What do you want, James?' she asked him coldly. 'As you can see——' she looked down pointedly at her dress '—I'm getting ready to go out.'

James looked down at her dress too, at the way the straight style emphasised the fullness of her breasts, the narrowness of her waist, the curve of her hips— and his expression warmed as it returned to the flushed loveliness of her make-up-less face. 'You look lovely, Silke,' he told her huskily.

She gave him a derisive look, her sigh impatient. 'I'm sure you didn't contact me again after all this time to tell me that!' she snapped.

'My marriage to Cheryl is over——'

'So?' Silke frowned up at him. 'What does that have to do with me?'

'I——' He broke off whatever he had been about to say as the telephone began to ring shrilly in the flat behind Silke.

Her mother! It had to be. 'I'm sorry, James.' She was becoming flustered again now. 'But, as you can see, this is hardly the right time for us to be talking— for whatever reason,' she added pointedly as he seemed about to protest. 'I have to go and take that call,' she told him agitatedly; the last thing she wanted was for her mother to ring off and then call back again when Lyon had arrived!

She didn't wait, hurrying back into her flat to hastily snatch up the receiver. 'Mummy?' she enquired anxiously—praying that it was!

'You sound out of breath, Silke,' her mother answered lightly. 'I didn't disturb you, did I?'

She had been disturbed since Lyon Buchanan had arrived at the agency this afternoon with the news that her mother was secretly about to marry his uncle! 'No, you aren't disturbing me,' she assured her mother, not even glancing round to see if James had left as she had asked him to. It was sad, really, that she had nothing to say to the man she had once intended marrying, but she really did have much more urgent things on her mind at the moment; namely Lyon's imminent arrival. 'Now what——?'

'One of us is here on the wrong evening,' remarked a smoothly arrogant voice across the room behind her. 'And I can assure you it isn't me!'

Silke closed her eyes, inwardly groaning, knowing exactly what she was going to see when she turned and looked across the room.

And she wasn't disappointed! James hadn't left at all, had moved inside the doorway of the flat, and standing beside him, looking arrogantly down his nose at the other man—he was several inches taller than James, Silke noticed inconsequentially—was Lyon Buchanan!

This was even worse than the nightmare at the agency this afternoon!

CHAPTER SEVEN

THE two men were eyeing each other up and down like two stags after the same doe, Lyon's face set in arrogantly forbidding lines as he looked at the other man with narrowed grey eyes, James frowning across at him with open dislike.

It was ridiculous. Absolutely ridiculous. Farcical, in fact. But it was happening right in front of Silke's eyes.

'Silke?' Her mother sounded puzzled by her sudden silence. 'Are you still there, darling?'

'No,' she answered dully, still watching the two men. 'And I have a feeling I won't be for some time,' she added heavily. 'Can you call back tomorrow?'

'No, darling, I can't,' her mother protested. 'I— Lyon isn't there again, is he?' she added disbelievingly as the idea obviously occurred to her—and she wondered what on earth he was doing at Silke's flat.

'Afraid so,' Silke answered drily. 'Just get back to me when you can. And good luck,' she added before putting the receiver down. No doubt her mother would be deeply puzzled by Lyon's presence here, but there was no way at this moment that Silke could even try to explain it!

The two men were dressed similarly, in dark suits and white shirts, but Lyon's suit was obviously of a superior cut, his shirt silk. And that was the only similarity between the two men, Silke realised as she looked across the room at them, one being so blond,

118

the other so dark, Lyon ten years older than the other man—and having all the assurance those years brought along with them. James had visibly started to wilt as the other man continued to look at him coldly.

'No one has the wrong night,' Silke said smoothly as she moved to join them near the door. 'James was just leaving.' She looked at him challengingly, having little sympathy for his discomfort in the face of the other man's arrogance; he had no right to come here at all, and it was his own fault if he wasn't exactly welcomed!

Impatient anger darkened the blue of his eyes at Silke's obvious dismissal—reminding her all too vividly of that temper she had forgotten during the year James was out of her life, a temper she had over-looked altogether whenever she allowed herself to think of him the last year. But she remembered it all too well now, also her attempts in the past to appease that temper James had inherited from his Scottish ancestors. Well, not any more!

'Weren't you?' she prompted as she held the door open pointedly.

The Cameron temper flashed again briefly in those expressive blue eyes before he quickly brought it back under control. He gave a distant nod. 'I'll call you tomorrow,' he told her evenly, not even sparing Lyon a second glance as he strode out of the flat.

Silke's hand was shaking slightly as she closed the door behind him. My God, she had just effectively thrown James out of her flat. And her life? But he wasn't in her life, she reminded herself forcefully; he was a married man, and of no interest to her whatsoever.

'James?' Lyon repeated softly, drawing her attention to him, his head tilted as he looked down at her with questioning grey eyes.

'You're early,' Silke accused impatiently, having no intention of satisfying his curiosity where James was concerned.

He shook his head. 'I arrived here at exactly seven-thirty,' he drawled derisively.

Silke looked down at the slender watch on her wrist; it was now seven thirty-five—where had the time gone?

'You really should learn to rotate your men in a more effective way,' Lyon added tauntingly at her obvious surprise at the time. 'Preferably choosing different evenings for seeing them!'

Silke's cheeks were flushed at his open mockery. 'James is not one of "my men"!'

'Meaning I am?' Lyon's brows were raised enquiringly.

'Of course not,' she snapped impatiently. 'I just meant that James was not expected here this evening at all.' If ever!

'James...' Lyon repeated softly again, thoughtfully. 'Would that be James Cameron?' he bit out with a forcefulness that had been totally belied by his earlier mildness.

Throwing her into a false sense of security! How did he know James's surname? She was sure she hadn't—of course, that damned report he had on her mother; it had told him of her engagement to James. And the subsequent breaking of that engagement, she was sure. Oh, God...! Her humiliation had been bad enough at the time; she certainly didn't need to be reminded of it by Lyon Buchanan, of all people.

Her head went back in a defiant gesture she couldn't quite control. 'If you'll excuse me, I'll go and finish getting ready.' She was still standing here in her dress and underwear and nothing else! God, no wonder he had thought—— But he had no right to think anything; she wasn't answerable to Lyon for her actions—no matter what they might be!

'No, I won't excuse you,' Lyon told her firmly as he reached out and grasped her wrist in a grip that was steely. 'You didn't answer my question. Was that James Cameron, your ex-fiancé?'

So he did know exactly who James was! 'And if it was?' Her cheeks were flushed with anger, her eyes flashing deeply green as she looked up into his coldly compelling face.

'He's a married man,' Lyon bit out harshly.

'Yes.' She still looked up at him defiantly. Why should she feel so defensive? She had done nothing wrong, and even if she had it was none of Lyon's business.

Lyon's eyes were icy as his gaze raked over her. 'And that doesn't bother you?'

'Why should it?' she returned dismissively. Because it did no longer bother her that James was married to someone else. For months after they had broken up she had tortured herself with thoughts of James as someone else's husband, but tonight she had realised it simply didn't matter any more, that she had stopped loving him a long time ago. If tonight had done nothing else, it had proved that to her.

Lyon's grip tightened about her wrist as he pulled her up against his chest. 'You were going to marry him once, and he married someone else,' he cruelly reminded her.

'We all make mistakes,' she dismissed again. 'Lyon, let me go!' Her pulse was starting to race, her body to tremble, at his close proximity.

He shook his head. 'I had started to believe I may have made a mistake about you,' he grated. 'But I guess not!' His head lowered, and that cruel twist of a mouth savagely claimed hers.

It was too much, all too much. First the worry of her mother and Henry, then her earlier confrontation with Lyon, James's unexpected visit here, and now this. It was just too much!

Lyon's mouth was moving against hers with a determination that owed nothing to passion and everything to a contempt for her he wasn't even trying to hide, his arms like steel bands as he moulded her body against the hardness of his, his hands running expertly up and down the curve of her spine.

Silke stood limply in his arms, offering no resistance but certainly none of the response she had known with him before either. How could she respond to what was no more than coldly clinical, a lesson in dominance that Lyon had every intention of winning? Only she wasn't playing; she felt numb from the angry onslaught.

Finally Lyon seemed to realise she was like a ragdoll in his arms, and he raised his head to look down at her, his eyes blazing with an emotion it was difficult to define, his mouth taut with anger. 'What is it?' he rasped harshly, his arms still holding her firmly against him. 'Has Cameron had all the response you're going to give this evening?'

She wanted to snap back, to be as angry as he obviously was, but the fight had gone out of her, all her defences crashing, even anger, as she realised, looking up into Lyon's harshly attractive face, that she was falling in love with him. With a man who had shown her nothing but anger and contempt since the moment they first met. It wasn't just stupid, it was insane; *she* was insane. But a part of her yearned to know the real Lyon, the child in Lyon that had been brought up by a man who had lost the woman he loved, the young man who had grown cynical because his wealth meant more to the women he met than the man himself, this older man who obviously saw women as people to be used as he himself had been used in the past. Oh, yes, Henry had talked to her about Lyon's childhood and his learned cynicism, but she wanted *Lyon* to talk to her about it, to tell her of all his pain, to... She *was* insane; Lyon would never talk to her of those things—because to him she was just another one of those women. Didn't what had happened just now more than prove that?

Something of her emotions must have shown in her face, and Lyon's expression was suddenly wary. 'Silke?' He frowned darkly.

'Oh, Lyon...!' She could have wept, for him, for herself. She was falling in love with a man who wasn't capable of feeling love for anyone, let alone the daughter of the woman he considered a gold-digger.

'Tears, Silke?' His frown deepened as he looked down at her searchingly. 'For Cameron?'

She hadn't realised there were tears, but now she was aware of them, warm against her cheeks. For whom? Herself? Lyon? Both, probably. God, what a mess!

'Answer me, Silke!' Lyon gripped the tops of her arms now, shaking her slightly. 'You still love him, is that it?'

'No,' she answered without hesitation, knowing that she didn't. How could she possibly love James when Lyon overshadowed him in every way? She had known that when she'd looked at the two men together earlier. Thank God she had never married James; and she had never thought she would ever say that!

'Then what is it?' He frowned. 'Did I hurt you?' He touched her lips with gentle fingertips, lips that were slightly swollen from his earlier kisses. 'God, I did,' he groaned in realisation of the damage his savagery had done. 'I never meant to hurt you, Silke.' He shook his head.

He was going to hurt her in a way he didn't even realise, couldn't be allowed to realise. 'It doesn't matter, Lyon,' she told him huskily, shaken by the gentleness of his touch against her mouth. God, don't let him be gentle now, not when she was already feeling so vulnerable towards him.

His expression darkened. 'Of course it damn well——' He broke off, drawing in a ragged breath, both hands cupping each side of her face now as he wiped the tears from her cheeks with his thumb-tips. 'I've never made a woman cry before,' he said gruffly.

Not to his knowledge, perhaps, but Silke was sure that not all the women that had entered and then left his life had done so with their heart intact. She couldn't be the only one who had wanted to know, and love, the man behind the cynical mask.

It was madness. This was Lyon Buchanan, the man totally opposed to her mother marrying his uncle, a man who had only contempt for her too, and not only as 'Satin's' daughter. But as she looked up at him all she could see was Lyon, the man she was falling in

love with. The man she so wanted to kiss her again,
but this time not with anger...

'Never,' he repeated huskily, a perplexed look on
his face.

Silke was powerless to move as his head lowered,
his mouth claiming hers, not roughly this time, but
with the same gentleness as his fingertips had touched
only seconds earlier. And Silke was lost...

The kiss of searching gentleness went on and on,
never-ending to Silke, her hands first clinging to the
broadness of his shoulders, and then moving caress-
ingly across his back before becoming entangled in
the curling thickness of the hair at his nape. Lyon
groaned deep in his throat at the intimacy as Silke's
fingertips brushed against the sensitive skin there as
she held him to her.

His mouth instantly became more demanding, the
tip of his tongue moving lightly against her inner lip.
Silke's mouth tingled from the caress, pressing more
closely against him as that tongue invaded her mouth,
invaded her, engaging in a duel with hers, a duel only
one of them could win. And as Lyon lightly cupped
one of her breasts with his hand Silke knew which one
of them it was going to be...

His thumb moved lightly over the fabric of her
dress, finding the nipple that pouted there, sensations
warming the whole of her body as he began a rhythmic
caress that made her ache with need.

And still his mouth possessed hers, his tongue telling
her of his own need, the hardness of his thighs pressed
against her, the muscles rippling across his back as
her hands moved beneath his jacket to caress him
through the silk of his shirt.

His mouth was against her neck now, kissing the pulsing column down to the sensitive hollow at the base of her throat, his breath hot against her burning flesh. And still he continued to caress her breast. Silke arched against him, totally lost to all reason, all sense but Lyon's touch and the feel of his hands against her body.

'God, I want you!' he suddenly groaned raggedly. 'I want you more than I've ever wanted anyone or anything in my life before!' He raised his head to look down at her with eyes dark with passion. 'Silke ... ?'

She knew what he was asking—and he didn't need to; her own need of him must be so obvious to him! But they were who they were, and——

'No,' he bit out firmly as he saw the hesitation in her eyes. 'We knew this would happen from the moment we first met. We both knew it.'

Had she? She had been very aware of him then, but as a man filled with anger, not——

'Silke ... !' he groaned again, his mouth nibbling at hers now, barely touching, asking, cajoling, tempting ... !

She couldn't think any more, didn't want to, only wanted this man, and the pleasure his caresses and kisses promised, wanted that with a hunger she hadn't known existed within her.

'Yes, Lyon,' she breathed against his mouth. 'God, yes!'

He swung her up in his arms as if she weighed nothing at all—which to him she probably didn't!—carrying her through the open doorway of her bedroom, laying her tenderly down on the bed, removing her clothes with the gentleness she had found so surprising in him after his initial savagery, until

Silke lay naked before him, unashamedly so, the creamy softness of her body smooth and unblemished, breasts pert, her stomach slenderly lovely, hips curved and inviting.

'You are beautiful,' Lyon murmured raggedly. 'Absolutely lovely!'

She knelt on the bed, revelling in the pleasure of helping him undress. She had known his body had to be as beautiful as those hands she found so fascinating, and was not disappointed when he stood unclothed beside her, dark hair covering that muscled chest on its path down to his thighs, not an ounce of superfluous flesh anywhere, his stomach taut, his need of her evident in his nakedness.

Nothing mattered to either of them now but pleasuring each other. And Lyon gave Silke pleasure as she had never known before, time after time, until she quivered with her need for his full possession, so desperately wanted him inside her, where she knew instinctively he belonged.

'Touch me, Silke,' he encouraged achingly. 'Help me. Guide me.'

He felt like velvet, and as he shuddered beneath her touch she knew they both wanted that velvet hardness inside her, sheathed inside her silky warmth, giving them both even more pleasure, pleasure undreamt of. And so she did as he asked, guiding him, groaning her protest as he would have stopped at the barrier that suddenly halted his progress.

'Silke?' He looked down at her with stunned disbelief.

'Don't go, Lyon,' she pleaded as he would have pulled away from her.

He shook his head. 'But you're a——'

'Not any more.' She took the initiative, arching up against him, looking up into his eyes as he breached that barrier, knowing only a brief moment of pain, and then that overwhelming pleasure returned as Lyon joined totally with her.

'You—oh, God...!' He ceased even trying to remain controlled as their bodies moved instinctively together in total harmony, bending his head so that his lips could claim a pouting breast.

And at the first touch of his mouth against her hardened nipple Silke felt the shudderings of an ecstasy she had never known before, wave after wave of pleasure taking her away from any reality but Lyon and their mutual lovemaking. Because Lyon was just as out of control as she was, tried desperately to be gentle still, but finally gave in to the primitive urge that was even stronger than he was, his mouth claiming hers even as he moved rhythmically inside her. And Silke knew that earth-shattering ecstasy once more before Lyon groaned his own pleasure, filling her, engulfing her.

Silke had often wondered how she would feel after making love for the first time. And now she knew. Awkward. Embarrassed. Apprehensive ... Maybe if it hadn't been Lyon who had made love to her she wouldn't have felt any of those things, certainly not the latter. But it was Lyon, a man she really hadn't known for very long, a man whom she loved but who didn't love her. A man who had been shocked by her virginity...

She had loved James, but, as they had always known they were going to marry, the question of their becoming lovers before that marriage hadn't really arisen. She had often asked herself, after James had gone off and married someone else, whether their lack of a physical relationship might have contributed to his going. Maybe it had. Although she doubted she would have known the ecstasy with him that she had just experienced. Lyon had known exactly how to make love to her to give her the ultimate in pleasure. And she hated the women who had given him that knowledge.

He lay on his back on the bed beside her, not touching her, not looking at her, staring up at the ceiling. Silke watched him beneath lowered lashes, wondering what he was thinking, but as usual his expression gave away none of his thoughts.

What happened now? How was she supposed to get through the next few minutes with any of her dignity intact? Or maybe she wasn't. This should never have happened——

'This should never have happened,' Lyon harshly echoed her thoughts even as he swung his legs off the bed to stand up and begin pulling on his clothes—clothes that had been strewn about the room in their haste to feel flesh against flesh. 'You should have told me,' he added accusingly once he had his trousers on and was tucking his shirt into the waistband with savage movements. 'This makes absolutely no difference to my dislike of your mother marrying my uncle, you know,' he told her coldly. 'I still——'

'Don't!' she warned harshly, all awkwardness and embarrassment gone. As for apprehension . . . ! 'Get out of here, Lyon,' she instructed coldly, getting up herself to pull on her grey silky robe to firmly tie the belt about her waist. 'And don't come back!' Her eyes flashed a warning at him not even to mention her mother and Henry again in connection with what had just happened.

He was fully dressed now, looking at her with narrowed steely grey eyes—looking nothing at all like the passionate, consumed man who had just made love to her! Maybe that was something else she had learnt today—you didn't have to be in love with the person you went to bed with. Because although she might have realised she was in love with Lyon, he certainly wasn't in love with her! How naïve she had been all these years to believe you actually had to love the person you made love with. But then it obviously hadn't been making love for Lyon but something much more ugly...

'I asked you to go,' she told him in a controlled voice. She just wanted to be alone, to try to salvage something from this situation. Starting with her pride.

'I still can't believe——' He gave a perplexed shake of his head. 'Silke, you and Cameron——'

'I don't want to talk about it,' she snapped dismissively. 'My relationship with James is nothing to do with you.'

'But you were going to marry the man.' Lyon frowned.

She looked at him challengingly. 'Yes?'

His frown deepened, and Silke could only imagine how she must look, her hair a blonde tangle about her face, her eyes wide, her mouth slightly swollen from the passion of their kisses. Just the thought of it made her face fill with heated colour and she could no longer meet his gaze.

'Never mind,' Lyon rasped harshly. 'Obviously, whatever happened—or didn't happen—between you in the past, Cameron has decided to renew the relationship!'

Silke's eyes widened. She had no idea why James had contacted her after all this time, but she certainly didn't believe it was for the reason Lyon did; James was married, and he had to know her at least well enough, after all this time, to realise she would never become involved with him again while he was a married man. She would never become involved with him again anyway!

Especially now... She had just made love with Lyon Buchanan, of all people!

'James can decide what he pleases; it really doesn't affect me,' Silke dismissed, walking to the bedroom door. 'I believe you were leaving,' she said again pointedly.

Lyon didn't move, fully dressed now, his dark hair slightly ruffled. From her fingers running through its silky thickness, Silke realised with an inward lurch of her stomach.

'We have to talk about what happened just now——'

'We don't have to talk about anything,' she cut in forcefully, wishing he would just leave so that she could lick her wounds in private. And she did feel very emotionally bruised, still couldn't quite believe what had happened between the two of them only minutes ago in this bedroom. She couldn't even look at the bed, didn't know how she was ever going to be able to sleep in it again without remembering Lyon being there. She didn't know how she was ever going to be able to sleep again anyway! 'We both know that—just now, was a mistake,' she added awkwardly.

'Maybe more of one than either of us realises. Yet,' Lyon concluded grimly.

Silke looked at him with puzzled eyes. How could it be more of a mistake than it already was? What— oh, no! She paled as she realised Lyon was referring to the possible consequences of what had just happened between them. But she couldn't be pregnant just from... Of course she could; she wasn't that naïve that she didn't know it only took the once to become pregnant. And because Lyon hadn't realised how innocent she was it hadn't entered his head—or hers!—to use contraception. Besides, she remembered with renewed embarrassment, she had taken matters out of his control and made that impossible for him.

She looked up at him, her eyes wide. 'You surely don't think that I deliberately——'

'Don't be so damned stupid,' he rasped harshly. 'Neither of us planned what happened between us just now—that's why we're in the predicament we are!' he added self-disgustedly.

Silke swallowed hard. 'We probably aren't in any predicament at all,' she dismissed with more confidence than she felt. God, what if she were to be pregnant? What would they—she—do? Would Lyon expect her to...? It wouldn't be any of his business, she decided firmly. It was her body, for goodness' sake; she could do what she liked with it—and that included giving birth to Lyon's child if she chose to do so. Just the thought of it made her stomach lurch!

'"Probably" doesn't do it, I'm afraid,' he bit out coldly.

'Well, for the moment it will have to, won't it?' Silke cut in heatedly. 'I'm not about to stand here now and discuss something that's *probably* not even a possibility.' She felt far too vulnerable standing here in her bedroom wearing only her silky dressing-gown, especially as Lyon was fully dressed. 'I suggest we just wait and see.' She walked to the bedroom doorway, pointedly waiting for him to leave, breathing an inward sigh of relief when he at last left her bedroom. Even if it was only to come to an abrupt halt in her lounge!

'I'll wait here for you while you dress for dinner,' he told her abruptly.

Silke gave a snort of disbelief. 'You aren't serious!' She stared at him.

'Would you rather I waited outside in my car?'

'I would rather you just left; I have no intention of having dinner with you now!' As if she could calmly sit across a table from him in a restaurant after what had just happened between them!

'We still have things to talk about, Silke,' he said grimly.

'We've already discussed the possibility of my being pregnant——'

'Not that,' he dismissed impatiently. 'That will become all too apparent in time. There's still the problem of your mother and my uncle.'

Silke frowned, looking at him searchingly. 'Is that the reason you invited me out to dinner?' she said slowly.

He gave a curt nod. 'The chances are they haven't actually gone through with the wedding yet, and——'

'I don't believe you,' she cut in forcefully, her hands clenched so tightly at her sides that her nails were digging into her palms. She had known there had to be a reason for his sudden invitation to dinner, but this! My God, did the man never give up? Obviously not. So much for his interest in seeing some of her jewellery designs in the right setting! 'I hope they have, Lyon. I hope they're already married and that there isn't a damn thing you can do about it!' She was so angry she could have hit him at that moment. 'Get out, Lyon. Just get out,' she added disgustedly.

'You——'

'Now, Lyon,' she told him through gritted teeth, her eyes flashing warningly.

He looked at her broodingly for several long seconds, finally giving an angry snort. 'You haven't seen the last of me, Silke, even if my uncle comes to his senses and decides not to marry your mother after all——'

'He'll marry her,' Silke said with defiant certainty.

He gave a dismissively disgusted shrug. 'Then that will be his problem. But the two of us now have unfinished business, Silke, and——'

'As far as you're concerned it's finished business, Lyon,' she cut in vehemently.

He shook his head, his eyes glacial. 'If there's a child I'll make it my business again, Silke.' He strode purposefully to the door. 'Count on it!' he warned before leaving, closing the door forcefully behind him.

It sounded more like a threat than a promise!

And, knowing Lyon as she did, it probably was. Oh, God, please let there not be any repercussions from her stupidity.

The stupidity of loving Lyon Buchanan...

CHAPTER EIGHT

IT HAD been a long and difficult week, a week when Silke had done a lot of soul-searching. She hadn't seen Lyon again since that evening at her flat, but the memory of it had never been far from her mind. In fact, it hadn't been out of it!

And the week certainly hadn't been helped by the fact that James had indeed 'called' her 'tomorrow'; in fact he had done better than that, he had telephoned her at the agency before coming there to see her in person. And what he had to say to her hadn't endeared him to her one little bit!

The only highlight of the week had been that her mother and Henry had actually managed to get married without any more interference from Lyon. A fact she was sure he was furious about! Not that the older couple looked at all troubled by that when they had returned from their honeymoon yesterday, the two of them obviously glowingly happy together.

But their return from their few days' honeymoon had been done deliberately Silke had learned last night, Henry informing her that there was a board meeting today—during which he intended proposing that Buchanan's look into the idea of introducing an exclusive jewellery department in their London branch!

Silke's answer to that had been a definite no. And no amount of arguing on Henry's part had managed

to persuade her otherwise. Much to Henry's chagrin.
He had accused her of being 'as stubborn as her
mother had been at eighteen!'.

But Silke had no intention of being accused of nep-
otism by Lyon. Besides, she was being kept busy
enough at the moment anyway. With her mother now
married to Henry she had little interest in running the
agency, wanted to spend time with her new husband,
making sure he didn't overdo things, and so Silke
could run the agency for her. Until such time as she
decided to sell it or close it down. And then Silke
would rethink her future. As far away from
Buchanan's as possible!

Silke had known that Henry was far from happy
with her refusal, but in the circumstances there was
really little he could do about it. She wanted to stay
as far away from Lyon in future as her mother's
marriage to his uncle would allow.

'So we're finally having dinner together.'

Silke drew in a deeply controlling breath. She hadn't
wanted to come to dinner with her mother and Henry
this evening at all, had guessed Lyon would be a guest
too, but had known she couldn't refuse when her
mother pointed out that it was their first dinner party
they had given together as husband and wife, and that
it would look very odd if her only child weren't
present. And so Silke had gritted her teeth and come
to the dinner party. Only to find Lyon had arrived
ahead of her, looking handsomely remote in a black
dinner-suit and snowy white shirt.

It had been easy to avoid talking to him as they
sipped their drinks before the meal, Henry eager to

introduce his new family to his friends. And Silke had been only too happy to fall in with this arrangement. Although she had been very much aware of Lyon's brooding presence in the room as she laughed and chatted with the other guests.

But as they all took their seats at the beautifully set dinner-table in her mother's new home, it became obvious she wasn't going to be able to ignore Lyon any longer; he was seated right next to her! It should have occurred to her that this might be the case, she now realised. After all, the other eight people here were all married couples; it was only natural, given the circumstances, that Lyon would be her dinner partner for the evening. She cursed the fact now that she hadn't asked if she could bring someone with her. Anyone!

She forced herself to look directly at him now, after having avoided doing so for the last half-hour. Although she had always known exactly where he was in the room, she acknowledged self-derisively. She had needed to know where he was so that she could avoid him!

But his mention now of 'having dinner together' only succeeded in bringing so vividly to mind the evening when they hadn't got as far as having dinner. Because they had ended up in her bed together instead!

She only hoped none of her inner turmoil at that memory showed as she coolly met his gaze. 'So we are,' she returned mildly, sitting back slightly as the avocado accompanied by prawns was placed in front of her.

Lyon waited until he had his own food before speaking to her again. 'Is that jewellery some of your own design?'

It had been the last thing Silke had expected him to say, and she almost choked on a prawn as she turned to look at him. Of all the things he could have said . . . ! What did it matter whether the chunky gold bracelet, earrings and necklace were her design; *the two of them had made love a week ago*!

But he didn't seem to be troubled by the same memories, was looking at the chunky bracelet on her wrist with cool interest. Well, maybe he just wasn't troubled by those memories; after all, it had hardly been the first time for him, had it? And any concern he might have had that it had been that for her seemed to have gone.

'Yes,' she finally confirmed tautly, swallowing hard, the prawn feeling as if it were stuck in her throat now. And she had the rest of the meal to get through yet—somehow!

She was hardly prepared for him to reach out to clasp her wrist with one of those beautifully tapered hands, lifting her hand towards him. Just the touch of his hand on her flesh was enough to make her want to wrench out of his grasp. It was an impulse she only succeeded in resisting with effort, forcing herself not to show any outward sign of her distress. Although she wasn't sure she had managed to hide the slight trembling of the hand he held . . .

'It's beautiful,' he murmured huskily, looking up suddenly, velvet-grey eyes holding her gaze.

Silke's breath caught—and held. What was he doing? She glanced about them self-consciously, but none of the other guests appeared to have noticed their exchange, either talking or already eating their food. Silke turned back to Lyon, swallowing hard.

'The bracelet,' he continued softly. 'It's beautiful.'

She had known he meant the bracelet! Of course she had! What else could he have meant? Certainly not her hand? She only hoped the warmth in her cheeks didn't give away the fact that briefly—very briefly!—she had thought that was exactly what he meant.

'Thank you,' she accepted distantly, firmly releasing her wrist before pointedly turning to the man who sat to her left, engaging him in lightly trivial conversation about the food. She couldn't have said anything more to Lyon at that moment if she had tried! And she didn't want to try, wanted a few minutes to collect her scattered wits.

Had Lyon done that deliberately? Did he know exactly how uncomfortable she felt about what had happened between them last week? She couldn't believe he didn't know, not in the circumstances. Was he playing with her? If he——

'How's James?'

Silke had been deeply lost in thought, her brief conversation over with the man seated to her left, but she looked up sharply at Lyon now, frowning.

'James,' he repeated lightly. 'How is he?'

She eyed him warily. 'James Cameron?'

Dark brows rose over mocking grey eyes. 'Is there another one?'

She wanted to say yes—she knew lots of men named James, but that would have been childish in the extreme. But what possible interest could he have in

James...? 'I believe he is very well,' she answered cautiously.

Lyon continued to look at her with that intently steady gaze. 'Don't you know?'

Silke managed a casually dismissive shrug. 'Why should I?'

He sat back in his high-backed dining chair. 'He's your friend; I thought you would know.'

'James isn't——' She broke off her angry rebuttal, drawing in a deeply controlling breath. The last thing James was was her friend. Or anything else. As Lyon should know only too well! 'That evening at my flat was the first time I had seen James for a year,' she told him defensively.

'You don't have to explain yourself to me, Silke,' Lyon said mockingly.

No, of course she didn't! Then why was she? Because he had engineered the conversation that way, that was why. Damn him!

She took several deep breaths, glad of the respite of the empty plates being cleared away to give her even more time to rebuild her defences against this man. Although if he continued to wrong-foot her in this way she didn't know how long that would last! She should never have come to this dinner party, should have found an acceptable excuse, no matter how disappointed her mother would have been. She simply wasn't ready to face Lyon yet. She didn't know if she ever would be!

'Except when it comes to who fathers my child,' he added grimly once they were alone again. 'And it won't be Cameron,' he bit out tautly, his relaxed demeanour gone now.

Silke gasped, looking about them self-consciously. But once again no one seemed to be paying any undue attention to them. Thank God.

She turned back indignantly to Lyon, undaunted by the grimness of his expression. So much for his earlier mildness; he had simply lulled her into a false sense of security!

'I'm not pregnant, Lyon,' she hissed firmly.

His eyes narrowed. 'You know that for certain, do you?'

No, of course she didn't. It was too soon. But she wasn't going to be. She couldn't be!

'I won't be,' she told him with certainty.

Lyon gave her a pitying look. 'If you are, you'll marry me.'

Silke stared at him, feeling the colour drain from her cheeks as she did so. He couldn't be serious! But one look at his determinedly set face and she knew he was. Very much so.

She shook her head. 'I wouldn't marry you——'

'I'm not the last man on earth, Silke,' he cut in mockingly. 'And it wouldn't matter if I were,' he added grimly. 'If you're having my child, I intend being its father. And not from a distance either.'

'This is ridiculous——'

'The whole situation is ridiculous,' he acknowledged harshly. 'Nevertheless, it exists.'

Silke felt ill, could see by the determined look on his face that he meant exactly what he said. And she already knew him well enough to know that there would be little escaping him if she did—by some terrible mischance!—happen to be pregnant. Oh, God! She might have fallen in love with Lyon, but she knew he certainly didn't love her, and any marriage made on those conditions had to be doomed to failure. Would be hell on earth, in fact.

She could feel the nausea rising up within her, knew she was seriously in danger of being sick as her next course of food was placed in front of her. One look at the beef—even beautifully presented as it was—and she knew it was no longer just a possibility, getting up hurriedly from the table to rush from the room, only just making it to the bathroom in time before losing the contents of her stomach.

'It's OK, Silke,' soothed an all too familiar voice as she stood with her burning forehead resting against the coolness of the mirror that covered the whole of the back wall of the bathroom. 'Here.' Lyon turned her gently round, placing a coldly damp facecloth against her forehead.

Silke just felt too ill at that moment to refuse his kindness, weak after her bout of nausea, resting limply against Lyon as he continued to hold the cool cloth against her face.

'Well, this wasn't quite the reaction I expected the first time I proposed marriage,' he murmured self-derisively. 'No,' he told her firmly, his arms tightening about her as she started to retch again. 'You——'

'Silke! Darling, what is it?' Her concerned mother entered the room, coming anxiously to Silke's side. 'Silke . . . ?' She smoothed the damp blonde hair from Silke's now pale face.

'Probably a prawn,' Lyon dismissed arrogantly before Silke could answer her mother. 'Don't worry about it, Tina, I'll take care of her.'

'Of course I'm worried about her,' her mother told him sharply before turning concernedly back to Silke. 'Darling, do you want to lie down for a while? Perhaps that——'

'I'll take her home,' Lyon cut in firmly, still holding Silke at his side.

'But——'

'You have your guests to attend to, Tina,' Lyon reminded challengingly. Lyon might have been presented with a *fait accompli* when Henry married his 'Satin', but it was obvious that he still didn't accept Tina Jordan as a suitable member of his family, and he wasn't hesitating now to remind her of her social manners; Silke may be ill, but as hostess of this dinner party her mother wasn't expected to abandon her guests in this way. A fact Lyon was reminding her of all too forcefully!

And he was right. The fact that Silke felt the way she did couldn't be allowed to interfere with her mother's first big social occasion as Henry's wife; Silke wouldn't allow that either.

'I'll be all right, Mummy,' she assured her mother weakly—feeling anything but all right. 'Please go back to the dinner party,' she added pleadingly as she could see her mother was about to protest further.

'I'll see that Silke gets home safely,' Lyon repeated firmly.

Silke could see her mother was still hesitating, and in truth Lyon was the last person she wanted to take her home—the last person she wanted to be with at all! He was the one who had made her ill in the first place!

'It's OK, Mummy.' Silke attempted to smile, knowing it hadn't quite come off, but it was the best she could do in the circumstances. 'As Lyon says, he'll see me home. Don't let this spoil your dinner party,' she encouraged with a lightness she was far from feeling. 'It must have just been something I've eaten,' she added dismissively.

'Not the prawns, I hope.' Her mother looked worried now. 'Can you imagine how awful it will be if all our guests come down with food poisoning?' She frowned. 'Not that it isn't dreadful enough if it's just you, Silke,' she continued hastily as she saw Lyon's mocking glance. 'It's just that——'

'I understand completely, Mummy,' Silke said drily, also having seen Lyon's mockery. 'And it happened too fast for it possibly to have been the prawns.' She gave Lyon a censorious look for having even suggested it could be that; he knew damn well how nervous her mother was about the success of this dinner party!

'Make our excuses, Tina.' Lyon took a firm hold of Silke's arm. 'I'll drive Silke home now. And stay with her until I think she's OK to be left,' he added challengingly.

It was a challenge Silke had no intention of taking up in front of her mother. But once the two of them were on their own it would be a different matter— Lyon wasn't staying at her flat with her for even a few minutes, let alone until she felt better. In fact, she doubted she could feel better until he was well away from her!

'Well, if you're sure...?' Her mother was looking at her closely, well aware of Silke's aversion to being in Lyon's company for any length of time. Even if she wasn't aware of the exact reason for it!

'Of course, Mummy.' Silke squeezed her hand reassuringly. 'I'm just sorry to have been so silly.' She gave a self-derisive grimace.

'You weren't being silly,' Lyon told her quietly as they left the house a few minutes later, a bright moon shining in the darkness outside. 'You were terrified,' he added with some amusement. 'Do you think I'll make that much of a despot of a husband?'

'You aren't going to be my husband!' Silke snapped, recovering some of her usual spirit, her initial shock over now, and the nausea having receded too.

Lyon raised dark brows as he unlocked the passenger door of his car for her. 'I didn't necessarily mean as a husband to you, I mean as a husband to any woman,' he drawled mockingly.

She swallowed hard. He was right, she had been terrified at the thought of marrying this man, but the thought of him as someone else's husband...! She suddenly felt sick again.

'Get in the car, Silke,' Lyon told her wearily as he saw her expression of abject misery—and completely misread it. 'Maybe you have eaten something that's disagreed with you, after all. You certainly look as if you're about to be ill again!'

She felt ill again. She couldn't marry Lyon, because he didn't love her, but the thought of him marrying someone else actually caused her a physical pain in her chest. Oh, God, this was a hopeless situation. How could she have fallen in love with someone so unsuitable, someone who couldn't possibly return her love?

She shook her head. 'I'll drive my own car.'

'Get in, Silke,' he told her in a voice that brooked no argument.

She glanced down at the leather seats. 'What if I'm sick again?'

'Then I'll have the car cleaned,' he dismissed with his usual arrogance. 'Oh, for God's sake get in, Silke,' he said impatiently. 'Otherwise we'll have your mother or Henry out here in a moment wanting to know what's going on!' He looked pointedly towards the house, the lights from the dining-room glowing out into the driveway, the people seated around the table perfectly visible to them—as they must be to them!

Silke got into the car, too tired now to argue any more. That was probably half the reason she had reacted as she had earlier and actually been physically sick; she hadn't slept at all well this last week, couldn't seem to stop thinking about her time in Lyon's arms. And its possible consequences!

'I can collect my car in the morning,' she told Lyon distractedly as he got into the car beside her.

'That's right, keep your independence to the last,' he bit out hardly, turning on the ignition, his face appearing to be chiselled out of granite in the eerie light coming up from the dashboard. 'If you're feeling better you can collect your car in the morning; other-wise——'

'Lyon——'

'Silke?' he returned in hard challenge.

She glared at him. 'I only agreed to letting you drive me home at all because I didn't want to upset my mother and Henry, I certainly have no intention of letting you tell me what I can or can't do now that we've left. I——'

'I'm well aware of the reason you agreed to my driving you home,' he cut in drily. 'And quite frankly I don't give a damn what made you agree; I would have carried you out of there kicking and screaming in protest if that's what it would have taken!'

He would have, too, Silke could tell that by his determined expression. God, how had she let herself become entangled with this man? How could she have let herself fall in love with him?

'At last,' he murmured several minutes later.

Silke looked at him wearily. 'Sorry?'

'I've rendered you speechless at last,' he softly taunted.

'Not exactly,' she snapped. 'And I haven't exactly noticed you're ever at a loss for words either!' She glared at him in the semi-darkness.

Lyon smiled. He actually smiled! A genuinely amused smile, without mockery, or any of those other cynical emotions Silke had come to associate with him. And in her already weakened state she could only wish he hadn't; he looked more attractive than ever grinning at her like that. And she didn't want to find him attractive, wanted to stay angry with him; it was her only defence at the moment.

'You would be surprised,' he finally murmured.

And just exactly what did he mean by that? Silke frowned. Certainly not that she had ever rendered him speechless. She couldn't think of a single occasion when he had been at a loss for... She gave a gasp in the darkness as she remembered all too well the one occasion when she had definitely rendered him speechless!

'Exactly,' he acknowledged softly beside her. 'That night was very special, Silke,' he added with husky gentleness.

She eyed him warily. It had been special for her, of course it had, but in what way could it possibly be special for him? 'Don't tell me,' she bit out angrily. 'I'm the first virgin you've ever taken to bed!'

'Silke——'

'Don't "Silke" me.' She was so upset now she was almost shouting in her agitation. 'You——'

'I didn't "take you to bed"; we made love to each other,' he cut in harshly. 'There's a distinct difference.'

'You should know!' she snapped forcefully. God, this was awful; she didn't want actually to talk about that night; she just wanted to try and forget it had ever happened. If she could. She certainly didn't want Lyon to tell her that night had been 'special' to him too!

How could it be 'special' to him? He was thirty-five years old, very attractive, must have made love to lots of women in the past.

His next words confirmed that. 'I'm ten years older than you, Silke,' he said almost gently. 'I'm certainly no innocent,' he acknowledged grimly. 'But neither do I take lightly what happened between the two of us last week.'

She stared straight ahead, her hands tightly gripping her small evening-bag. 'You've already made your feelings of responsibility perfectly plain,' she bit out tautly.

'Is that what you think it is?' He frowned.

'Of course,' she dismissed scathingly.

'I don't——'

'Look, Lyon, could we just drop this subject?' she said wearily. 'I have a headache now too, and I really don't want to think about this any more. I'll have enough explaining to do to my mother in the morning, without this!' she added resentfully.

The silence that followed this outburst wasn't exactly comfortable—but it was certainly preferable to their conversation! She had known she shouldn't have gone to the dinner party, had guessed it would be a disaster as far as she was concerned—she just hadn't realised how much of one it would be! She just wanted to go to bed now, go to sleep, and hope this whole situation—and Lyon!—would go away.

There didn't seem much chance of Lyon proving co-operative to her wish once they reached her flat, as he insisted on coming in with her, to make sure she was 'all right' before he left. She wasn't going to *be* OK until he had had left!

'I'll make you a hot drink,' he offered once they were inside her flat, looking around him for the kitchen. 'You go and get into bed and I'll bring it into you.'

He wouldn't have any trouble finding the bedroom, knew all too well where that was!

'I'm not an invalid, Lyon,' she snapped—although in truth she wanted nothing better than to crawl into bed and go to sleep; she still felt awful. 'I have no intention of going to bed.' Not until after he had left, anyway!

Lyon looked at her with a steady grey gaze. 'Tea or coffee?' he asked quietly.

Just go, she wanted to scream at him. 'I told you——'

'Tea or coffee?' he repeated firmly, challenge in his expression now.

She gave a frustrated sigh. 'Whatever,' she said wearily, shaking her head. Arrogant, arrogant man. 'The kitchen is through there,' she pointed to the door on their left.

He nodded abruptly, not showing by so much as a twitch of the eyebrow his satisfaction at once again achieving his own way. Which was just as well—Silke would probably have hit him if he had looked in the least triumphant. But then he probably knew that too!

'Go and get into bed,' he told her again, walking with long strides towards the kitchen.

Silke's frustration with the situation increased as she stood in the middle of her lounge listening to the sounds of him going through the cupboards, looking for the makings of the tea. If she didn't soon sit or lie down she had a feeling she was going to fall down, but the thought of Lyon bringing her a cup of tea in bed——! Oh, damn it, what did it matter? They weren't likely to leap on each other just because she was in bed. In fact, they weren't likely to leap on each other at all!

One glance in the bathroom mirror at the paleness of her face, the dark shadows under her eyes more visible against that pallor, and Silke knew she had nothing to worry about; she looked ghastly, not in the least alluring!

She bathed her face in cold water before getting herself ready for bed, already safely under the covers by the time Lyon came into the bedroom with the tray of tea things. And two cups, she noticed as he put the tray down on the bedside table.

'I had trouble finding the sugar,' he explained the length of time it had taken him to make the tea.

Silke was still eyeing those two cups on the tray. 'I don't take sugar,' she told him distractedly.

'But I do, in tea,' he said arrogantly, pouring the tea into the two cups before adding a liberal amount of sugar to one of them.

Silke watched him over the top of the bedclothes. He looked slightly incongruous standing there with the teapot in his hand, pouring tea into two delicate china cups; Silke couldn't help wondering if he had ever done anything like this in his life before.

Dark brows rose over quizzical grey eyes as he turned to look at her. 'What are you smiling at?'

She hadn't realised she was smiling, but she could feel the grin on her lips now, straightening her expression with effort. 'You do like sugar in tea,' she dismissed lightly, having no intention of telling him what she had actually been grinning at; he had actually looked quite endearing carrying out the mundane task of pouring tea for them both! Lyon—endearing; the two just didn't go together!

One brow rose sceptically at her explanation, but he didn't question her further on the subject. 'Sit up,' he instructed abruptly. 'You can't drink your tea flat on your back like that.'

She had deliberately lain 'flat on her back' so that she could have the bedclothes up to her chin, but of course he was right, she couldn't drink tea like this, not with any degree of success anyway!

His mouth twitched with humour as she sat up to reveal the print on her cotton nightshirt; the pig pattern was hardly sexy, she ruefully acknowledged. But she was very fond of the busy pig pattern—and she certainly didn't want to look sexy!

'Trying to tell me something?' he drawled, sitting on the side of her bed to drink his own tea.

Silke wished he hadn't done that; the last thing she needed was to have him close to her like this. But as he continued to sip his tea he showed every sign of being comfortable exactly where he was. Comfortable was the last thing she felt herself; she was unnerved by this intimacy, her hand shaking slightly as she lifted her own cup to her lips.

'Hardly,' she answered him dismissively. 'I wouldn't presume to tell you anything!'

His eyes warmed with humour. 'I don't think sarcasm becomes you!'

'I wasn't——' Her cheeks were slightly flushed. 'Perhaps I was,' she admitted ruefully.

He took her empty cup out of her hand, putting it back on the tray with his own, before making himself more comfortable on the bed. 'You look about ten years old with your hair brushed back like that, no make-up, and wearing that nightshirt!'

Her inner turmoil at his closeness wasn't that of a ten-year-old! She only wished it were. He looked so attractive in the black dinner-suit and white shirt, was so close she could smell that elusively tangy after-shave he wore. As for his hands, she refused to look at them!

'Your daughter would be beautiful, Silke,' he said huskily.

Her eyes widened. Daughter? Oh, no, he wasn't back on that subject! She couldn't——

'*You're* beautiful, Silke,' he added softly.

He was too close now, his head bending towards her, his lips only inches from her own. Silke's gaze was fixed on the beauty of that mouth, remembering all too well the emotions his kisses had evoked in her last time. Last time? God, she couldn't seriously be contemplating letting him kiss her again, not after what had happened between them last week! Letting him kiss her—she knew all too well that if Lyon decided to kiss her then it wouldn't be a case of 'letting' him do anything; Lyon was a law unto himself.

'Cameron was a fool.' His warm breath stirred her silky fringe. 'How could he have been engaged to you and not made love to you?' He shook his head disgustedly.

His mention of James was enough to free her of the sensually mesmerising spell he had been casting, and Silke drew back abruptly—she hadn't realised until that moment that she had half moved up from the pillow to meet his kiss!

But talking about James was enough to put a dampener on anything, reminding her all too forcefully of the meeting she had had with him in her mother's office last week. He had 'made a mistake' marrying Cheryl, he claimed, explaining that the marriage was now over, that he now realised he still loved Silke. And then he had asked her if they couldn't try again, if the two of them couldn't marry, as they had once planned, once his divorce from Cheryl was through!

Silke had been astounded at his cheek, that he had thought he could just walk back into her life, with the declaration of still loving her, and expect her to welcome him back. With open arms, apparently!

Needless to say she had told him exactly what he could do with his suggestion, had advised him to go back to his wife and try to make his marriage work. He had been furious at her lack of understanding, that Cameron temper quickly showing itself once he realised she wasn't about to fall back into his arms. Silke had been speechless at his nerve in even thinking he could come back to her after the way he had walked out on her a year ago—but she had quickly regained her voice when she ordered him to leave. And not to come back! His silence since that day seemed to confirm that he had taken her at her word. Thank goodness! It was up to him whether or not he took any notice of her advice about his marriage; as long as he stayed away from her she didn't care what else he did.

And she certainly didn't want to talk to Lyon about him now, in any context. 'I would like to go to sleep now, Lyon, if you don't mind,' she told him distantly, not really caring whether he minded or not; she just wanted him to leave.

His gaze narrowed on her thoughtfully—and what he read in her glittering green eyes must have warned him not to push her any further at the moment, because he straightened before standing up in preparation of leaving.

Silke moved uncomfortably under the intensity of that steely gaze, but her own gaze didn't drop, meeting his steadily as she willed him to just go.

'I'll take the tray back out to the kitchen,' he gave an abrupt nod—as if he had just come to an inner decision. 'Can I get you anything else before I leave...?'

'No,' she answered forcefully. Why didn't he just go and leave her in peace!

'OK,' he accepted smoothly. 'I'll see you in my office at nine-thirty on Monday morning, then——'

'What?' Silke sat up abruptly in the bed as she frowned at him.

'Our appointment is for nine-thirty on Monday——'

'What appointment?' Her frown deepened. What on earth was he talking about now?

Lyon studied her closely, obviously seeing her complete puzzlement at his statement. 'Did you get a chance to talk to Henry this evening?' he said slowly.

'Not privately, no.' She shook her head, her expression wary now. What had Henry been up to now?

'Ah.' Lyon nodded understanding. 'In that case I suggest you call him in the morning and——'

'I'm asking you now, Lyon,' Silke cut in agitatedly. 'What appointment? What possible reason could I have for coming to see you on Monday morning?'

His mouth twisted. 'To discuss your jewellery designs, of course.'

'My——?' She gasped. 'But I told Henry——'

'Get some sleep, Silke,' Lyon advised firmly. 'Everything will look better by Monday morning.'

Silke watched open-mouthed as he left without offering any further explanation. Not that one was necessary. Despite all her protests it was obvious Henry had gone ahead with his proposal for her

jewellery designs to be introduced to Buchanan's—
and it looked as if, in spite of the objections she knew
must have come from Lyon, Henry might have got
his own way!

Great. Just great!

Did no one ever listen to her?

Well, maybe they hadn't up until now. But they
were certainly going to on Monday morning!

CHAPTER NINE

'ENJOYING your swim?'

That was exactly what she had been doing! Had been. Lyon's arrival was sure to spoil that.

Her mother had decided to go into the agency today, insisting Silke take the day off, that she needed a little rest and relaxation after being ill on Saturday evening. Henry had offered her the use of his indoor pool in the grounds of their home, an offer Silke had been only too happy to accept. Until a few seconds ago, that was!

She had been floating aimlessly on her back in the water for the last twenty minutes or so, was enjoying the almost tropical warmth of the beautiful indoor pool, plants and loungers around the spacious pool adding to that effect. But at the first sound of Lyon's voice she had rolled self-consciously on to her front, swimming to the side now as he stood there watching her.

He looked slightly overdressed in his dark three-piece business suit and pale blue shirt, and con-sidering the heat in here he must be feeling slightly uncomfortable. Not that he looked it, just as arro-gantly self-assured as usual as he stood looking down at her.

'It's a beautiful pool,' she answered him warily, conscious of her slicked back hair and make-up-less face. She hadn't envisaged feeling at quite such a disadvantage the next time she saw him, hadn't for one moment imagined he would interrupt her leisurely swim. But then, when had Lyon ever done anything she expected him to do! Even so...

'Henry told me you were here,' he drily answered the question that had been forming on her lips.

Damn Henry. Didn't her stepfather realise that Lyon was the main stress and strain she was trying to escape from by taking up her mother's suggestion that she take the day off? Probably. One thing she was absolutely sure of since coming to know him better: that 'irresponsible old devil' pose Henry adopted was just that—a pose. He invariably knew exactly what he was doing. Just as he did this time. He wanted his own way just as much as he protested Lyon always did.

'We had an appointment at nine-thirty,' Lyon reminded her when she made no response.

'I cancelled it,' she told him dismissively as she climbed the marble steps out of the pool, all the time trying not to hurry her movements and show how uncomfortable she felt dressed in only her brief black bikini, her body lightly golden against the dark material. As quickly as she could without appearing too obvious she pulled on the white towelling robe Henry had provided, wrapping a towel about her wet hair before turning to face Lyon again.

And as she looked at the light mockery in his expression she knew that her efforts had all been wasted; he knew exactly how uncomfortable she had felt emerging from the pool in his presence. Damn him as well as Henry!

'I'm well aware of the fact that you cancelled the appointment,' Lyon drawled softly. 'So I thought I would come and see you instead,' he added challengingly.

'The "mountain coming to Mohammed"?' she derided, settling herself down on a white lounger, relieved to do so, as unnerved as she usually was to be in this man's company.

His mouth twisted. 'Something like that. Is the water warm?'

Silke looked up at him frowningly; what did the temperature of the water have to do with their conversation about her broken appointment?

'Is it?' he persisted.

'Very,' she answered distractedly.

'In that case——' he took off his tie, undoing the top button of his shirt '—I think I'll go in for a swim too.'

Silke blinked up at him. 'You don't have a costume,' she stated the obvious.

Dark brows rose over mocking grey eyes as he looked down at her. 'I always have one here for my use,' he told her tauntingly. 'Don't worry, Silke; I wasn't about to go skinny-dipping!'

Colour darkened her cheeks at his mockery; it was just like him to realise that had been her immediate worry!

'We can talk once I've had my swim,' he added arrogantly.

'I was thinking of leaving,' Silke told him stiffly, still smarting from his derision. But there was no way she could have sat here calmly while he swam naked—and she knew he was arrogantly sure enough of himself to have done exactly that if he felt like it!

He turned slowly back to look at her. 'Henry told me you intended spending the day here...?' He arched questioning brows.

Damn Henry; exactly what was he up to? He knew how much she wanted to avoid Lyon's company, and yet he had told the other man where she was, and how long she intended staying here.

She shrugged. 'I have things to do.'

'They can wait,' Lyon told her arrogantly. 'At least until after I've had my swim and we've talked,' he added drily as she would have protested at his autocratic manner.

Silke glared after him as he went to get changed. Arrogant, arrogant...God, he was so infuriating; she was starting to repeat herself now!

What could he want to talk to her about? Not her jewellery designs, surely? He had made his feelings clear right from the beginning concerning her mother's motives for marrying Henry, had classed her in the same category. But he had seemed more than a little interested in the jewellery she had been wearing on Saturday...

'Why so pensive, Silke?'

She had been so deep in thought that she hadn't been aware of his return, her eyes widening as she looked up at him standing next to her lounger, swallowing hard as she took in the male beauty of him. Brief black swimming trunks covered the lower part of his body, a body that was tautly muscled, covered in a fine dark hair, the skin lightly tanned. He was breathtaking!

'Silke?' he prompted softly as she continued to stare at him.

She blinked, shaking her head slightly to break the spell of his mesmerising virility. But it wasn't easy to do. She had made love with this man, her body pressed against his, his arms like steel bands about her as he claimed her. And as she looked at him she wanted him again. Oh, God...!

He reached out to remove the towel from about her hair, loosening the silky blonde strands down on to her shoulders, his fingers gently caressing, his gaze intent on her flushed face.

Oh, God, could he see the desire in her face? Was her need of him there in her eyes?

'Are you coming in for another swim?'

It had been the last thing she'd expected him to say, and her breath left her lungs in a sigh—her first indication that she had been holding her breath in the first place! She swallowed hard. 'No, I—I think I'll just sit here for a while,' she refused awkwardly, not sure if her legs would support her if she should attempt to stand up!

Lyon looked down at her searchingly. 'Are you still feeling ill?'

She shook her head, the damp tendrils of hair cold about her flushed face. 'I had been swimming for almost an hour when you arrived,' she dismissed the suggestion—although she did feel slightly weak-kneed in this man's presence!

He nodded, straightening, at last removing his hand from her hair—and allowing Silke to breathe once again! 'I won't be long,' he assured her—before diving neatly into the clear water and swimming towards the opposite end of the pool with evenly strong strokes.

He could stay in the water for the rest of the day as far as Silke was concerned; that way she might be able to relax her jangled nerves, and force herself to breathe easily! He really was the most infuriating——! No, he wasn't infuriating, she admitted heavily; she was just in love with the man—which had to be worse!

What was she going to do about her feelings towards this man? What *could* she do? He was Henry's nephew, had been brought up as the son the older man had never had, and with Silke's mother's marriage to his uncle Lyon was going to be in her own life for a long time to come. Which was going to be like hell on earth!

She had, in fact, spent much of the weekend and this morning thinking what she was going to do about the situation. And she hadn't come up with any solutions, other than actually moving away from the area completely, possibly even going abroad somewhere. Maybe if she went to America she might be able to get somewhere with her designs. It was the only really feasible idea she had come up with so far, but it seemed a little drastic even so.

'You are pensive, aren't you?' Lyon frowned as he sat down on the lounger next to hers, towelling the darkness of his hair dry as he did so.

Silke forced a lightness to her expression. 'Deep in thought,' she corrected dismissively.

'Concerning what?' Lyon still watched her intently.

She gave a light laugh. 'Really, Lyon, you're being extremely rude; aren't a person's thoughts supposed to be the one thing that is completely private?'

He gave a rueful smile. 'I thought we had both agreed that I am "extremely rude"; so what were you thinking about?'

She couldn't very well say, 'You!' 'The future,' she shrugged. 'I have a few decisions to make.'

'About Cameron?' he bit out, his eyes narrowed, the white towel about his neck now as he sat forward on the lounger.

Silke gave an impatient sigh. 'I thought I told you James means nothing to me; he certainly doesn't come into any of my plans for the future!'

Lyon nodded dismissively. 'Good!' he said with satisfaction. 'Then what are these plans? No,' he added firmly. 'Before you tell me what you're thinking of doing, let me tell you of the offer Buchanan's wants to make to you.'

'No!' She sat up abruptly, dark green eyes flashing a warning. 'I don't want Buchanan's to "make me an offer"——'

'Buchanan's—or me?' he grated harshly.

'Aren't they one and the same?' she challenged.

'Possibly,' he conceded softly.

'Definitely,' she said with feeling. 'And less than two weeks ago you believed I was nothing but a little gold-digger who intended marrying your uncle for what I could get! The fact that it was my mother who married Henry instead doesn't change that fact, and I have no intention of accepting anything from you or Buchanan's!'

'It's not a question of accepting anything——'

'Yes, it is,' she interrupted with feeling. 'What happened between us last week hasn't helped the situation either.' Colour darkened her cheeks even as she mentioned the subject.

His mouth tightened. 'This offer has nothing to do with that!'

'Doesn't it?' she scorned. 'I doubt very much that's true. You had absolutely no interest in my designs until then.'

'I hadn't seen any of them then!' Lyon rasped, eyes lightly grey.

'You haven't seen any of them now!' Silke returned heatedly. 'The set I was wearing on Saturday is not enough for you to base a serious decision like this——'

'I'm a businessman, Silke,' he cut in harshly. 'I never make business decisions lightly. Of course I've seen other of your designs, as have the rest of the board. And we all agreed that——'

'Just a minute,' she interrupted softly, holding up a silencing hand. 'When did you see any other of my designs?' She looked at him searchingly.

He returned that gaze just as searchingly, the anger and suspicion in her face unmistakable. 'Hmm,' he finally murmured. 'I have a feeling we have a serious problem here.'

Silke's gaze didn't waver. 'When did you see other of my designs, Lyon?' she repeated evenly, the flashing of her eyes belying that calmness.

He shrugged. 'Last week. At the board meeting. All the board saw them.'

'And just how did my designs get into your board meeting, Lyon?' she asked steadily. But she knew. Of course she knew!

How dared they? And she knew it had to be 'they'; Henry might have the arrogance to present her designs to Buchanan's board without her permission, but she didn't for one moment believe he had been the one to acquire them from her flat in the first place. Her mother had to have been involved in this too. And Silke was furious at their interference in her life in this underhand way.

Lyon drew in a deeply controlling breath. 'Henry didn't have your permission to show them, did he?' he said slowly, eyes narrowed thoughtfully on her flushed face.

'Of course he didn't,' she snapped. 'I told him exactly what I thought of the idea of my designs being introduced at Buchanan's!'

Lyon nodded. 'Because you genuinely don't believe your designs are good enough—or because of me?'

The colour deepened in her cheeks. 'Of course my designs are good enough——' She broke off abruptly, her gaze challenging as she saw the derision in his face at her admission of its being him that was the problem.

Well, she would be lying if she claimed otherwise; no one in their right mind, in normal circumstances, would pass up the opportunity to market their jewellery designs in a prestigious store like Buchanan's. And she might not be a lot of things, but she was definitely in her right mind. But these were not normal circumstances, and she had no intention of using her new family connection to achieve that end.

'So it's me,' Lyon said softly.

'Not for the reason you think!' she denied heatedly.

Dark brows rose over silver-grey eyes. 'And what reason do I think?' he challenged evenly.

'Look, Lyon——' she stood up, moving away from him, needlessly tightening the belt on her towelling robe '—I don't feel like playing games——'

'I'm not playing games, Silke.' He had stood up too, was now standing dangerously close behind her. Dangerously. Because when he was this close to her Silke couldn't even think straight, let alone try and match him in a verbal way. 'Why am I such a problem to you?'

'You aren't a—problem—to—me...' She had spun round to vehemently deny the claim—only to then realise just how close Lyon was, standing only inches away from her now, Silke staring up at him with widely apprehensive eyes.

He reached out to touch the heat of one of her cheeks with cool fingertips. 'I don't think that's exactly true, Silke,' he murmured huskily. 'And you're certainly a problem for me,' he added gruffly.

She swallowed hard, mesmerised by his darkly powerful face. 'I am?' she said breathlessly, completely unable to move away from the caress of his hand.

'You are,' he nodded, his gaze locked with hers.

She moistened suddenly dry lips—instantly stopping the action when she saw how his gaze darkened at the movement. 'Why?'

He gave a half-smile, slightly self-derisive. 'You've been a problem for me since the moment I first saw you at the store in that ridiculous bunny girl costume!' He shook his head at the memory.

Silke still cringed at the thought of that day. 'I can't go on apologising for that mistake for the rest of my life——'

'I wasn't asking you to apologise,' Lyon dismissed lightly. 'I don't think you——'

'Am I interrupting something?'

Silke spun round self-consciously at the sound of Henry's voice, realising as she saw the speculation in curious grey eyes how damning the situation must look with Lyon and herself standing close together like this, Lyon's hand still resting against her cheek, a cheek now grown even warmer in her feeling of awkwardness.

'I thought I might join the two of you for a swim,' Henry continued drily, holding up his towel as proof of his claim. 'But I can see I'll just be in the way,' he added with some amusement.

It was totally the wrong thing for him to say as far as Silke was concerned. After what he had done last week, how dared he come in here talking in that indulgently patronising tone, implying—well, just implying! The last thing she wanted was for Henry to get the wrong impression about Lyon and herself; she would never hear the end of it, from either Henry or her mother.

She moved pointedly away from Lyon, deliberately not looking at him now either, although she could sense his gaze on her. She glared at Henry. 'You aren't in the way at all, Henry,' she bit out tautly. 'In fact, you're just the person I wanted to see!'

'Oh, dear,' he grimaced, frowning. 'I recognise that light of battle in your eyes, Silke; you look just the way your mother did at eighteen.'

'I probably feel the same way my mother did at eighteen!' she snapped impatiently. 'You undoubtedly walked all over her feelings too!'

Henry's frown deepened. 'What have I done now?'

'I should take care if I were you, Henry,' Lyon drawled, stepping back—as if he were about to stand back and enjoy watching the show. 'You're standing on very shaky ground. And, actually, in this case, I happen to agree with Silke,' he added seriously.

She looked at him in surprise. 'You do?'

His mouth quirked with humour. 'I do,' he confirmed drily.

She gave him a frustrated glare before turning away to look at Henry again, the anger still in her face. 'You and Mummy had no right to take my designs out of my flat——'

'Ah,' Henry gave a guilty grimace. 'But Silke, we were only thinking of you,' he added in a cajoling tone. 'Your designs are brilliant; I don't know why someone hasn't snapped them up years ago. And——'

'Stop the flattery, Henry,' she cut in forcefully. 'You had no right doing what you did without my permission!' Her eyes flashed deeply green.

'It's probably a criminal offence,' Lyon put in softly.

It was his uncle's turn to glare now. 'You stay out of this, Lyon,' Henry snapped.

'Just pointing out a relevant fact,' Lyon shrugged, the amusement still in his eyes.

'Just enjoying yourself, you mean,' his uncle accused in a disgruntled voice.

Lyon gave another dismissive shrug, moving to sit on one of the loungers. 'Don't mind me,' he invited lightly, looking up at the two of them as Silke and Henry faced each other across the pool like adversaries.

Which, as far as Silke was concerned, at this moment, they were. But, nevertheless, she had no intention of putting on a show for Lyon. No matter how angry she was with Henry!

'I have no intention of even discussing this further,' she bit out tautly, that angry flush still in her cheeks. 'I think what you and Mummy did was despicable,' she told Henry with feeling.

'I agree,' Lyon put in softly.

'And as for you——' Silke turned on him furiously '—I don't even want to hear the offer you were going to make me! We both know it actually has nothing to do with my designs, and neither of us owes the other anything just because of what happened between us last week.' She was breathing hard in her deep agitation.

What Lyon was doing was tantamount to 'payment for services rendered'—an obligation he felt because of her innocence before that night!

'What happened between the two of you last week?' Henry put in curiously.

Silke looked at him with stricken eyes, realising exactly what she had done; Henry was nothing if not determined, and she doubted he would let this go now that he sensed there was more to Silke's relationship to Lyon than either he or her mother could have possibly guessed. But that was Lyon's problem. She was getting out of here, as far away from these two men as possible!

But before she could make a move, Lyon spoke. 'Mind your own business,' he told the older man coldly.

'But——'

'Stay out of this, Henry.' Lyon stood up, turning to Silke now, the coldness leaving his expression. 'Silke, we——'

'There isn't a "we",' she told him heatedly. 'Not a business "we", and certainly not a personal one! Just leave me alone!'

'Silke——'

'I said leave me alone, Lyon,' she bit out vehemently, her hands clenched into fists at her sides. 'Just stay away from me. Both of you!' she warned before turning and running from the poolside.

And she wanted to keep on running and never stop!

CHAPTER TEN

'HELLO, Silke.'

'Go away, Lyon.' She closed the door back in his face, wishing she had never opened it in the first place; she should have guessed who it was ringing her doorbell! She had only returned from Henry's house just over an hour ago; she should have realised that Lyon's arrogance wouldn't allow him to be dismissed in the angry way she had done.

But Lyon moved quicker than she did, putting his foot inside the door, making it impossible for her to completely close it, a determined expression on his face.

Silke stood her ground, keeping the door closed as far as it would go. 'I said go away, Lyon,' she told him forcefully.

He met her gaze steadily, his expression grim now. 'I want to talk to you,' he bit out harshly.

Her head went back defensively. 'And it must be obvious that I have nothing to say to you.'

Lyon shook his head. 'We have a lot to say to each other.'

'I don't think so,' she bit out tersely.

'Silke——'

'Please go, Lyon,' she said, more desperately this time; if he didn't go away soon she was going to cry.

She had left Henry's house earlier as if the devil were on her heels, had just wanted to get away from both men. And she didn't feel any more like dealing with Lyon now than she had then; she needed time to herself, to think, to try to sort out what she was going to do with her life. One thing she did know: she couldn't stay on here in London; she would have to make a complete break, otherwise she would never be free of seeing Lyon. And having to constantly deal with her feelings for him.

'For God's sake let me in, Silke,' he muttered as her neighbour across the hallway came out of his flat, the man looking at them curiously as he did so.

It irritated her that she was being manipulated in this way, but she accepted they must look rather odd, her standing so defensively in her half-open doorway, Lyon so arrogantly demanding on her doorstep.

She opened the door reluctantly, moving back into her sitting-room. Two minutes, she promised herself, and then he was going to leave again. Anything they had to say to each other could be said in that time!

'You're going away.' Lyon bit the statement out harshly.

She turned almost guiltily, groaning inwardly as she saw that she had left her bedroom door open, her open case on the bed, clothes strewn across the bed as she haphazardly decided what she was going to take away with her. She had decided on the drive back home that she would have to go away for a couple of days anyway, just to distance herself from this whole situation. And from the look on Lyon's face he wasn't at all pleased at the idea of her going anywhere. Tough!

'Yes,' she answered challengingly. 'I——' She broke off as the doorbell rang. If that was her mother or Henry——!

Lyon looked far from pleased at the interruption too, glaring after Silke as she went to answer the door. As she opened the door and saw who her visitor was Silke knew he was going to be even more furious. She wasn't too pleased herself!

Not again! She couldn't believe this; she hadn't seen James for a year, and now he had appeared at her door twice in a week—and both times Lyon had been here too. And Lyon would never believe it was simply coincidence. Though what did it matter what Lyon believed? It was none of his business who chose to visit her!

'Hello, Silke,' James greeted slightly awkwardly. 'I just——'

'You again!' Lyon rasped accusingly, having moved to stand just behind Silke without her having been aware of it, looking arrogantly over the top of her head at the other man now, cold anger in glittering grey eyes. 'Don't you have a wife to go home to?' he added challengingly.

Silke gasped at his bluntness—but then, when had Lyon ever been anything else? 'Lyon, I don't think——' she began.

'No, you obviously aren't thinking at all,' he bit out contemptuously, his mouth curled back in a half-sneer. 'You lied to me earlier, Silke,' he said coldly. 'It's obvious now exactly who you're going away with. You silly little fool, don't you realise——?'

'Hey, I don't think you should be talking to Silke like that,' James gave a perplexed frown.

'You stay out of this,' Lyon told the other man with dismissive arrogance, eyes glittering a warning before he turned to Silke. 'When you come to your senses, my offer may no longer be available,' he warned her harshly.

Her head went back defensively. 'Which offer would that be?'

His mouth tightened. 'Both of them!'

'I'm not interested in either of them!' She shook her head, meeting his gaze with steady determination.

He glanced contemptuously at the still slightly puzzled James, before turning back to Silke. 'I just hope you know what you're doing,' he bit out forcefully, shaking his head—as if he were absolutely sure she couldn't possibly know.

'I know exactly what I'm doing, Lyon,' she told him with certainty. 'Now, if you wouldn't mind, I have my packing to finish,' she added pointedly.

He drew in a harshly angry breath. 'God, Silke, you——'

'Goodbye, Lyon,' she cut in firmly; if he didn't soon leave her legs were going to buckle beneath her and she was going to collapse in a heap on the carpet at his feet!

He gave James a coldly quelling glare before looking back at Silke. 'Your family will still be here for you when you decide you need them again—which I don't think will be too far in the future!' he added with another disgusted glance in James's direction.

'My family!' She almost choked over the statement; a week ago this man had been fighting any connection with her at all; now he claimed to be part of her family! The man was incredible!

'Yes, family, Silke,' he echoed challengingly.

Silke couldn't be bothered to argue with him any more, especially in front of James; but 'family' was the last thing she considered Lyon to be. And he must have a very short memory himself if he really thought he could claim that! And she knew damn well there was nothing wrong whatsoever with Lyon's memory.

'Goodbye, Lyon,' she said almost wearily.

'Is there nothing I can say to make you change your mind about this?' His tone had softened slightly. 'Silke, you know what happened before, and the situation is so much worse now. Please think about what you're doing.' The last was added almost gently.

She knew he believed her to be going away with James, and she could see how displeased he was at that idea, and part of her wanted to tell him that she wasn't doing that at all. But the sensible side of her knew it would achieve nothing, that she had to go away anyway, and perhaps it was better, for the moment, to let Lyon go on believing she was leaving with James. She would tell her mother the truth, obviously, wouldn't let her worry unnecessarily.

'I've thought, Lyon,' she told him huskily. 'And this is what I want.'

His mouth tightened again. 'Very well,' he bit out harshly before walking to the door. But he didn't leave straight away, stopping in front of James, looking coldly at the younger man. 'Take care of her, Cameron. Or this time you'll have me to answer to,' he added ominously.

Silke frowned after him as he finally left. Part of her had been resentful of his slightly possessive tone. The rest of her had felt the warmth of her love for him. And it was the latter she had to fight now; Lyon didn't love her, just felt he had some sort of proprietorial right to her because of what had happened between them.

She suddenly became aware of James's curious look, and attempted to shake off her gloom concerning Lyon as she returned James's gaze.

He grimaced. 'Bad timing again!'

Her mouth twisted. 'You could say that.'

James nodded. 'Who is that man?'

She stiffened. 'Is it important?'

He shrugged. 'Not if you don't want to tell me. And why should you?' he dismissed self-derisively. 'I actually only called round to tell you that Cheryl and I are all right again now. After last week I thought I owed you that at least,' he added sheepishly. 'You must think I'm a complete idiot!'

'Come in, James,' she invited wearily, wondering how she had ever thought this man was strong and capable; he had behaved like a hurt little boy this last couple of weeks, wanting to get back the toy he had given up because the one he really wanted had decided not to play for a while. 'Can I get you a cup of tea or something?' she offered once he had come in and closed the door behind him.

'No, thanks. Cheryl will be expecting me home soon,' he added with a self-conscious grimace.

Silke nodded. 'I'm glad the two of you have sorted things out.'

'I behaved like an idiot last week, didn't I?' He sighed. 'It's just that things were so awful between Cheryl and me, and then I began to wonder if I hadn't made a mistake giving you up, and——'

'It really doesn't matter, James,' she cut in dismissively. 'There's no harm done. Either with me or Cheryl,' she added ruefully.

'I was obviously wasting my time with you.' He nodded.

Silke gave him a sharp look. 'What do you mean?'

He gave her an affectionate smile. 'You love that man Lyon, don't you?'

'No, I——' She broke off her vehement denial as James gave her a look of teasing reproval. 'Maybe,' she conceded tautly.

James grinned at her now, obviously elated at having his marriage back again, his avowals of love for Silke only a week ago completely forgotten, and his anger at her rejection too. 'Not maybe, Silke, definitely!' he teased. 'And he obviously feels the same way——'

'No, he doesn't,' she cut in determinedly.

'No?' James questioned derisively. 'Then why does he act like a jealous lover every time he sees me?'

Colour warmed her cheeks at having Lyon described as her lover. Because that was what he had been. Her only lover.

'Ah,' James said knowledgeably.

Silke looked at him frowningly. 'What do you mean, "ah"?'

He shook his head. 'I really am sorry for behaving like an idiot last week, Silke.' He walked to the door. 'Send me an invitation to the wedding, won't you?' he added teasingly as he prepared to leave. 'It probably wouldn't be a good idea for me to come, but at least the invitation will tell me the two of you have sorted things out. And I would like to think of you being happy, Silke,' he added huskily.

'Not with Lyon,' she told him firmly, shaking her head.

'We'll see,' he returned enigmatically. 'And the first thing you ought to do is let him know that you aren't going away with me!'

She had no intention of telling Lyon any such thing. He would learn the truth soon enough, no doubt, but for the moment she needed a little breathing space. Time to get away. Time to get over loving Lyon...

'What are you doing, darling?' Her mother looked at her concernedly as they sat across from each other in the spacious sitting-room of her new home.

Silke had called in briefly to talk to her mother before going away; she didn't want to cause her mother any more distress than she had had in recent weeks, by simply disappearing. Obviously Lyon had seen her mother first!

'Not what Lyon thinks I am,' she answered drily.

'You and Lyon...' her mother began slowly, a slightly puzzled frown on her face.

Silke stiffened. 'There isn't a "Lyon and me",' she denied determinedly.

Her mother looked at her closely. 'Oh, I think there is,' she said knowingly.

She shook her head. 'No, I——'

'Silke, I've talked to Lyon,' her mother put in quietly.

Silke gave her a sharp look. What did she mean, she had talked to Lyon? What about? Surely he wouldn't have—— No, she didn't believe for one moment Lyon would have told her mother what had happened between them.

'We've *both* talked,' her mother corrected herself. 'About the past, about my meeting Henry again after all these years. I think—no, I'm *sure* Lyon understands what happened now.'

Silke watched her closely. 'And?'

'And we understand each other better now,' her mother smiled. 'It's because of that understanding——' she sobered '—that I don't think history should repeat itself.' She gave Silke a pointed look.

She stiffened, at once on the defensive. 'I don't know what you mean,' she avoided. There was no chance of history repeating itself; she might love Lyon, but he certainly didn't love her.

'You're running, Silke,' her mother chided. 'Just as I did. Don't you think you should give Lyon a chance?'

'To do what?' she frowned.

'Silke, I don't know what this business with James is all about, but I do know you aren't going away with him, as Lyon thinks you are.' She shook her head.

Silke frowned. 'Lyon told you about that?'

'I told you.' Her mother nodded. 'We talked. About all sorts of things.'

'Such as?' Silke was defensive again now; what if Lyon had told her mother about their intimacy?

'Silke, why did you let him go on believing you're going away with James?' her mother persisted, not answering her question.

'Because——' To her chagrin her voice broke. 'Because at the time I just wanted him to leave,' she finished more firmly.

'Why?'

'Mummy——'

'This is important, Silke,' her mother cut in determinedly. 'I wasted thirty-five years; I have no intention of seeing you make the same mistake.'

Silke blinked back the tears, her control going now, her hands twisted tightly together in her lap. 'Because if he hadn't left when he did I would have broken down,' she admitted shakily. 'Because I love him,' she said more forcefully, shaken at putting her feelings into words for the first time. 'Because he doesn't love me!' she choked, the tears starting to fall now, blinding her as she buried her face in her hands.

'He loves you, Silke,' an all too familiar voice told her huskily. 'He just isn't very good at admitting he loves anyone. Basically because I didn't want to love anyone,' Lyon admitted gruffly.

Silke had turned, stricken, at the first sound of his voice, staring at him dazedly as he stood in the open doorway. How long had he been standing there? She hadn't even realised he was here; his car hadn't been outside in the driveway when she arrived, and——

Had he just said that he loved her?

'I think I'll leave the two of you alone together,' her mother stood up. 'Thirty-five years is a long time, Silke,' her mother reminded her softly, squeezing her arm as she walked past her to leave the room.

Lyon watched Silke from across the room, dark and attractive in a navy silk shirt and navy fitted trousers, his expression wary now, a little uncertain. It wasn't an emotion Silke would ever have associated with him!

She stood up slowly, smoothing her hands down her denim-clad thighs. 'I had no idea you were here,' she said nervously, her eyes wide as she looked at him.

'I came down with your mother earlier,' he shrugged. 'As she said, I wanted to talk to her.'

Silke nodded. 'I'm glad the two of you have sorted out your differences, that you've decided to accept my mother in your uncle's life.'

The two of them were talking to each other like strangers; maybe she *had* imagined that he had said he loved her?

'I think it may be a question of the other way around,' Lyon gave a self-derisive grimace. 'I realise now what your mother must have gone through all those years ago,' he explained at her questioning look. 'She had more reason to resent me rather than the other way round. If Henry hadn't been made my guardian the two of them would have been married years ago!'

Her mother and Lyon *had* done some talking, hadn't they? 'Possibly,' Silke acknowledged. 'But they both put that in the past, and so I think you should too.'

He nodded. 'That's what your mother said,' he told her ruefully.

The two of them continued to look at each other, neither of them speaking, neither of them moving, just looking at each other. And it was killing Silke. *Had* he said he loved her?

'Of course I love you,' he spoke huskily—and Silke realised she had said the words out loud!

Her cheeks felt hot as she stared at him. 'I love you too,' she finally said softly.

'So what are we going to do about it?' he prompted abruptly.

Silke gave a shaky laugh, hardly able to believe this conversation was taking place. 'Whatever we want to do, I suppose,' she spoke huskily.

'I want to marry you,' Lyon told her evenly.

This was ridiculous! They had just said that they loved each other, Lyon had told her he wanted to marry her—and yet they still faced each other across the width of the room as if they were adversaries!

'Marriage is a trap,' she said, reminding him that he had once told her it was a trap he had no intention of getting into.

He shook his head. 'Not when you love the person you marry,' he said firmly.

'I now know for certain I'm not pregnant, Lyon,' she told him almost regretfully; when she had thought she would be going out of his life for good it had been some comfort to think she might, just might, be expecting his child. Now she knew that was no longer a possibility.

'Not yet, perhaps,' he accepted gently. 'But we have plenty of time to have children. If you'll marry me?'

He looked uncertain again—and it was an emotion Silke didn't like to see in him. His arrogance might have angered her in the past, but it was Lyon, and to see him like this was almost too difficult to bear.

'I might—if you'll come over here and kiss me!' She looked at him teasingly beneath lowered lashes.

He gave a throaty chuckle, walking towards her. 'I thought you'd never ask!' he groaned as he took her in his arms, crushing her against the lean length of him, burying his face in her silky hair.

Her arms were about his neck, her body moulded to his. 'You don't usually wait to be asked,' she teased huskily.

'The new me,' he said with self-mockery as he raised his head to look down at her. '*Will* you marry me, Silke?'

Her face was raised to his, her face glowing; it was going to be all right. It really was! 'You haven't kissed me yet,' she reminded lightly.

'Once I start I might not stop,' he admitted self-derisively. 'So maybe you had better give me your answer first!'

'Yes,' she said without hesitation. 'Yes, yes, yes!'

He gave a triumphant laugh before sweeping her up into his arms and carrying her over to the sofa— where he proceeded to kiss her until they were both breathless!

'I fell in love with you the moment you removed that ridiculous bunny head,' he told her some time later, Silke nestled in his arms as she sat next to him on the sofa.

'You didn't,' she protested, looking up at him. 'You were absolutely horrible to me that day.'

'I didn't want to love you,' he reminded huskily. 'But Henry has told me that he fell in love with your mother on sight all those years ago, and I'm afraid I did the same thing with you.'

'"Afraid"?' she teased, touching the hardness of his cheek with caressing fingers.

'Hmm.' He gave a self-derisive grimace. 'And if Henry hadn't collapsed in the way that he did, and diverted attention away from the situation I suddenly found myself in, I might have made a complete idiot of myself.'

'Not you, Lyon,' Silke lightly mocked. 'You're far too controlled.'

'My control went out of the window that day, too!' he admitted ruefully. 'The Jordan women are pretty powerful stuff!'

'The Winter-Buchanan men too,' she smiled up at him lovingly.

Lyon returned the warmth of her smile, smoothing the silky hair at her brow. 'A mutual admiration society, hmm?'

'Not to start with,' she reminded him reprovingly. 'You really were awful to Mummy and me.'

'I didn't want you in my life.' He grimaced. 'I had lived without love in my life for so long, and I didn't want it there then either.'

'And now?' Silke kissed the length of his jaw.

'Now I wish we were already married and I could take you away somewhere and make love to you without interruption,' he admitted huskily. 'But I doubt either Henry or your mother would let us get away with that; it will have to be the whole "white wedding" bit!'

She looked up at him searchingly. 'Not if that isn't what you want.' She shook her head. 'I was going to have that once before, and it isn't important——'

'Silke.' He looked down at her intently now. 'I want to see you walking down the aisle to me in a silky white gown, want to watch with pride as you become my wife. Cameron was an idiot,' he grimly repeated the accusation he had made once before concerning James.

'I was never going away with him, Lyon,' Silke assured him. 'I only let you go on believing that so that you would leave.'

He nodded. 'I realise that now.'

'James's marriage had been going through a rough patch, and he—well, he thought——'

'I don't give a damn what he thought.' Lyon's arms tightened about her possessively. 'Now that I know you love me, he isn't coming anywhere near you ever again!'

But she would send James his wedding invitation, just so that he would know she and Lyon had 'sorted things out', and that she was going to be happy; she knew James would have enough sense not actually to attend the wedding!

'I don't *want* him anywhere near me again,' she dismissed lightly. 'I didn't want him near me on the two occasions you did see him.'

'Good,' Lyon said with satisfaction. 'It totally threw me when I realised he was back in your life,' he acknowledged ruefully. 'But it certainly took my mind off Henry and your mother.' He grimaced. 'Their relationship suddenly took second place in my priorities!'

'It didn't seem that way,' Silke frowned. Although, thinking about it, perhaps Lyon had become less intense about Henry and her mother after seeing James at her flat that evening...

'Quite honestly——' Lyon gave a rueful smile '—Henry could have married a twenty-five-year-old bunny girl after that and I wouldn't have objected!' He looked down at her teasingly.

Silke gave a soft laugh. 'You're not going to let me forget that incident in a hurry, are you?' She hugged him for the sheer pleasure of being able to do so; she loved this man with every part of her. And the miracle was, he loved her in return.

'When I'm Henry's age I'll be telling our grand-children about the way we first met!' he warned her affectionately.

She didn't doubt he would too. And just the thought of those children and grandchildren was enough to fill her with a warm glow for their future together.

'Our children will grow up in a loving family, Silke,' he assured her huskily, looking deeply into her eyes. 'There will be none of the loneliness for them that we both knew in our own childhoods. They will have two parents who love them. And, more importantly, who love each other,' he added with satisfaction.

And they did love each other. Very much. And they would continue to do so. Silke didn't doubt it for a moment, knew that neither of them had fallen in love lightly. And it was a love that would last a lifetime.

The war was over at last. And both of them had won . . .

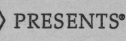

MILLION DOLLAR SWEEPSTAKES (III)

No purchase necessary. To enter, follow the directions published. Method of entry may vary. For eligibility, entries must be received no later than March 31, 1996. No liability is assumed for printing errors, lost, late or misdirected entries. Odds of winning are determined by the number of eligible entries distributed and received. Prizewinners will be determined no later than June 30, 1996.

Sweepstakes open to residents of the U.S. (except Puerto Rico), Canada, Europe and Taiwan who are 18 years of age or older. All applicable laws and regulations apply. Sweepstakes offer void wherever prohibited by law. Values of all prizes are in U.S. currency. This sweepstakes is presented by Torstar Corp., its subsidiaries and affiliates, in conjunction with book, merchandise and/or product offerings. For a copy of the Official Rules send a self-addressed, stamped envelope (WA residents need not affix return postage) to: MILLION DOLLAR SWEEPSTAKES (III) Rules, P.O. Box 4573, Blair, NE 68009, USA.

EXTRA BONUS PRIZE DRAWING

No purchase necessary. The Extra Bonus Prize will be awarded in a random drawing to be conducted no later than 5/30/96 from among all entries received. To qualify, entries must be received by 3/31/96 and comply with published directions. Drawing open to residents of the U.S. (except Puerto Rico), Canada, Europe and Taiwan who are 18 years of age or older. All applicable laws and regulations apply; offer void wherever prohibited by law. Odds of winning are dependent upon number of eligible entries received. Prize is valued in U.S. currency. The offer is presented by Torstar Corp., its subsidiaries and affiliates in conjunction with book, merchandise and/or product offering. For a copy of the Official Rules governing this sweepstakes, send a self-addressed, stamped envelope (WA residents need not affix return postage) to: Extra Bonus Prize Drawing Rules, P.O. Box 4590, Blair, NE 68009, USA.

SWP-H395

HARLEQUIN®

PRESENTS Plus

"Virgin or wanton?" Oliver Lee is suspicious of everything and everyone.... When he meets Fliss, he thinks her innocence is an act. Fliss *may* be innocent, but the passion Oliver inspires in her is just like raw silk—beautiful, unique and desirable. But like raw silk it is fragile....Only love will help it survive.

Ben Claremont seemed to be the only man in the world who didn't lust after Honey's body...but he asked her to marry him anyway! Honey wasn't in love with him—so separate rooms would suit her just fine! But what on earth had she gotten herself into? Were their wedding vows based on a lie?

Presents Plus—the Power of Passion!

Coming next month:

Raw Silk by Anne Mather
Harlequin Presents Plus #1731

and

Separate Rooms by Diana Hamilton
Harlequin Presents Plus #1732

Harlequin Presents Plus
The best has just gotten better!

Available in April wherever Harlequin books are sold.

Harlequin invites you to the most
romantic wedding of the season.

Rope the cowboy of your dreams in
Marry Me, Cowboy!

A collection of 4 brand-new stories,
celebrating weddings, written by:

New York Times bestselling author

JANET DAILEY

and favorite authors

Margaret Way
Anne McAllister
Susan Fox

Be sure not to miss Marry Me, Cowboy!
coming this April

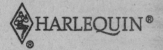

If you enjoyed this book by

CAROLE MORTIMER

Here's your chance to order more stories by one of
Harlequin's favorite authors:

Harlequin Presents®

◆ HARLEQUIN®